## "Actions speak louder than words. And what you're doing is ignoring me and Rose."

"I'm not ignoring the baby, I'm ignoring *you*."

"Why?" Lilah demanded, tossing both hands high.

Could she really not see what it cost him to avoid her company? Was she clueless about the attraction sizzling between them? Well, if so, Reed thought, it was time to let her know exactly what was going on here.

Her scent reached for him, surrounded him and he threw caution out the damn window. "Because of this."

He grabbed her, pulled her in close and kissed her as he'd wanted to for days.

\* \* \*

*The Baby Inheritance* is part of Mills & Boon's no.1 bestselling series,

**Billionaires and Babies:**
Powerful men… wrapped around their babies' little fingers.

# THE BABY INHERITANCE

BY
MAUREEN CHILD

First Published in Great Britain 2016
By Mills & Boon, an imprint of HarperCollins*Publishers*
1 London Bridge Street, London, SE1 9GF

© 2016 Maureen Child

ISBN: 978-0-263-06497-1

Our policy is to use papers that are natural, renewable and recyclable
products and made from wood grown in sustainable forests. The logging
and manufacturing processes conform to the legal environmental
regulations of the country of origin.

Printed and bound in Great Britain
by CPI Antony Rowe, Chippenham, Wiltshire

**Maureen Child** writes for the Mills & Boon Desire line and can't imagine a better job.

A seven-time finalist for a prestigious Romance Writers of America RITA® Award, Maureen is an author of more than one hundred romance novels. Her books regularly appear on bestseller lists and have won several awards, including a Prism Award, a National Readers' Choice Award, a Colorado Romance Writers Award of Excellence and a Golden Quill Award. She is a native Californian but has recently moved to the mountains of Utah.

To Patti Canterbury Hambleton—Best friend
since first grade and still the absolute *Best*.

For all the laughs and tears and crazy adventures.

I love you.

# One

"Divorce is reality," Reed Hudson told his client. "It's marriage that's the anomaly."

Carson Duke, America's favorite action-movie star, just stared at his attorney for a long minute, before saying, "That's cold."

Reed shook his head slowly. The man was here to end a marriage that most of the country looked on as a fairy tale come to life, and still he didn't want to accept the simple truth. Reed had seen this over and over again. Oh, most of the people who came to him were *eager* to end a marriage that had become inconvenient or boring or both. But there were a few people who came to him wishing they were anywhere but in his office, ending a relationship that they'd hoped was forever.

*Forever.* Even the thought nearly brought a smile. In his experience, both business and personal, there was no such thing as *forever.*

"Like I said," Reed told Carson with a shake of his head, "not cold. Reality."

"Harsh." Then Carson snorted a short laugh and crossed his legs, his ankle on top of his knee. Frowning a little, he asked quietly, "You ever been married?"

Now Reed laughed. "Oh, hell, no."

Just the idea of him ever getting married was ridiculous. His reputation alone, as what the tabloids called the "divorce attorney to the stars," was enough to make sure no woman he was involved with developed long-term plans. And representing most of Hollywood and New York in high-profile divorce cases had all started with a single client five years before. Reed had represented television's most likable comedian in a nasty split from a wife who made the "bunny boiler" look like a good time.

Word had spread in Hollywood and across celebrity lines, and soon Reed's practice was littered with the rich and famous. He enjoyed his work, relished protecting his clients from bad relationships and shattering the occasional prenup. And, if there was one thing he'd learned through the years, it was that even the best marriage could dissolve into misery.

But, he hadn't exactly needed his clients to teach him that lesson. His own family was a sterling example of just how badly marriages could go. His father was now on wife number five and living in London, while Reed's mother and husband number four were currently enjoying the heat and tropical atmosphere of Bali. And from what Reed had been hearing, his mother was already looking for husband number five. Thanks to his serially monogamous parents, Reed had ten siblings, full and half, ranging in age from three to thirty-two with another baby sister due any minute thanks to his father's ridiculously young, and apparently fertile, wife.

For most of his life, Reed, as the oldest child in the wildly eclectic and extended immediate family, had been the one who stepped in and kept things moving. When his siblings had a problem, they came to him. When his parents needed a fast divorce in order to marry their next "true love," they came to him. When the apocalypse finally arrived, he had no doubt that they would all turn to him, expecting Reed to save all of their asses. He was used to it and had long ago accepted his role in the Hudson clan. The fact that his experience as a mediator had served him so well as an attorney was simply a bonus.

Looking at his latest client, Reed thought back over the past year and remembered the innumerable articles and pictures flashed across the tabloids. Carson Duke and his wife, Tia Brennan, had graced the covers of magazines and the pages of newspapers, and the two had been favorites on the celebrity websites. They'd had a whirlwind romance that had ended in a fairy-tale wedding on a Hawaiian cliff overlooking the Pacific.

Stories proclaiming the nearly magical connection between the two, holding them up as examples of what "real" love looked like, had been printed, pored over and discussed all across the world. Yet here Carson sat, a little more than a year later, hiring Reed to represent him in a divorce that promised to be as high-profile as the marriage had been.

"Let's get down to business then," Reed said and looked at the man across from him. Just like in his movies, Carson Duke looked tough, determined and had the cool, hard gaze of a seasoned warrior. Not surprising, since the star had been a US Marine before turning to Hollywood. "First tell me what your wife thinks about all of this."

Carson sighed, shoved one hand through his hair and then blurted out, "It was her idea. Things have been rough between us for a while now." It looked as though every word he spoke tasted bitter. "She—*we*—decided that it would be better, for both of us, if we just end the marriage and walk away now, before things get ugly."

"Uh-huh." Duke sounded reasonable, but so many of Reed's clients did when they were first entering the muddy swamp of litigation. Couples determined to remain "friendly" eventually succumbed to name-calling and vicious diatribes. Reed wasn't looking forward to watching Carson and his wife go down that path. "I need to know—are you seeing someone else? Is another woman at the bottom of all this? I will find out sooner or later, so it would be better for all of us if you tell me now so there are no surprises."

Carson stiffened, but Reed held up a hand to silence what would no doubt be a tirade of insult and outrage. All of his clients tended to paint themselves as the injured party, and if Reed wasn't careful, he could be blindsided by a scorned lover testifying for the opposition. Better to have as much information as possible from the jump. "These are questions I have to ask. If you're smart, you'll answer."

Carson stewed in his chair for a second or two, looked as though he'd like to punch something, then surged to his feet in one smooth motion.

"No," he snapped, and paced across the room to stop at one of the wide windows overlooking the sweep of ocean stretching out into the distance. He stared through the glass for several long seconds, as if trying to calm down, then turned his head to look directly at Reed. "No. I didn't cheat. Neither did Tia."

Reed's eyebrows arched. First time he'd heard a client *defend* a spouse. "You're sure about her?"

"Absolutely." Carson shook his head and looked back through the glass at the sunlight dancing on the ocean's surface. "This isn't about cheating or lying or any other damn thing."

Intriguing. The old *irreconcilable differences* plea was usually just an excuse to keep secrets private. There were always reasons for a divorce, and in Reed's experience, cheating was right at the top of the list.

"Then why are you here?" Reed asked, leaning back in his black leather desk chair.

"Because we're not happy anymore." Carson laid one hand on the glass. "It started out great," he continued as if to himself. "Tia and I met and it was like…magic. You know?"

"No," Reed said, smiling. "But I'll take your word for it."

Carson shook his head. "We couldn't keep our hands off each other. From that first moment, there was something powerful between us." He smiled, and shot Reed another quick glance. "It was more than sex, though. We used to talk all night, laughing, planning, talking about moving out of Hollywood, having kids. But the last few months, between work and other demands on both of us…hell. We hardly see each other anymore. So why be married?"

Pitiful excuse to sentence yourself to divorce court, but then, Reed silently acknowledged, he'd heard worse. He'd once represented a man who claimed he needed

a divorce because his wife kept hiding cookies from
him. Reed had almost advised him to buy his own damn
cookies, but had figured it was none of his business. Because the cookies weren't the real reason. They were
simply the excuse. The man wanted a divorce; Reed
would get it for him. That was his job. He wasn't a marriage counselor, after all.

"All right then," Reed said briskly. "I'll get the paperwork started. Tia won't be contesting the divorce?"

"No." Carson shoved both hands into his pockets.
"Like I said. Her idea."

"That'll make it easier," Reed told him.

Wryly, Carson whispered, "I suppose that's a good
thing."

"It is." Reed watched his client and felt a stir of sympathy. He wasn't a cold man. He knew that people came
to him when their worlds were dissolving. In order to
maintain a professional distance, he sometimes came
off as harsh when all he was trying to do was to be a
rock for his clients. To be the one stable point in a suddenly rocking world. And as he studied Carson Duke,
he knew the man didn't need pity, he needed someone to
guide him through unfamiliar waters. "Trust me," Reed
said. "You don't want a long, drawn-out battle described
daily in the tabloids."

Carson shuddered at the idea. "I can't even take the
trash out at my house without some photographer leaning out of a tree for a picture. You know, on the drive
down here from Malibu, I was telling myself that it'd
be a hell of a lot easier on most of us if your office was
in LA—but getting away from most of the paparazzi is
worth the drive."

Over the years, Reed had told himself the same

thing about relocating to Los Angeles many times, but damned if he could convince himself to move. A quick glance around his office only reinforced that feeling. The building itself was old—built in 1890—though thankfully it had been spared the Victorian gingerbread so popular at the time. He'd bought the building, had it completely remodeled and now, it was just as he wanted it. Character on the outside, sleek and elegant on the inside, plus the office was only a fifteen-minute drive from his home.

Besides, Reed preferred Orange County. Liked the fact that Newport Beach sprawled out in front of his two-story building crouched on the Pacific Coast Highway and he had the majestic sweep of ocean behind him. Sure, in the summer the streets were crowded with tourists—but he'd have the same problem in LA without the beautiful setting. Newport Beach was more laid-back than LA, but upscale enough to convince clients they were with the right attorney. Besides, if he had to drive the 405 freeway every night to get from his office to his home at the Saint Regis hotel in Laguna Beach, he'd be spending more than two hours a night just sitting in traffic. If clients wanted the best, then they'd better be ready to do the drive.

"I'll have the papers drawn up and messengered to you in a few days."

"No need," the other man said. "I'm taking a few days. Staying at the Saint Regis Monarch. I've got a suite there."

Since Reed lived in a massive suite at the exclusive, five-star resort, he knew the hotel would give Carson the distance he wanted from Hollywood and the scoop-hungry photographers who would be hunting him once news of an impending divorce hit the media. And it would hit, no matter how they tried to keep it quiet. If Carson or Tia's people didn't release the news, then someone along the chain of information would. There were always leaks no matter how hard you tried to keep things confidential. It wouldn't come from Reed's staff, that he knew. They were paid extremely well—not just for their expertise, but for their discretion—and knew their jobs depended on their ability to keep their clients' business to themselves.

But there were others out there Reed had no control over. Everyone from valets at the Monarch to desk clerks and hotel maids. Once the media found out where Carson was staying, they'd continue to dig until they found out why the action star was holed up sixty miles from his house.

"You live at the Monarch, don't you?" Carson asked.

"Yeah, I do. So once the paperwork is completed, I'll have it all sent to your room for signing."

"Convenient, huh?" Carson said wryly. "Anyway, I'm registered under the name Wyatt Earp."

Reed laughed. The wildly famous usually signed into hotels under false names to keep those *not* in their immediate circle from knowing where they were. "Got it," he said. "I'll be in touch."

"Right." Carson nodded. "Thanks, I guess."

Reed watched the man go and once the office door was closed again, he walked to the windows behind his desk and stared out at the view of the ocean as his client had done only moments ago. He'd been through this so many times now, with so many people, he knew what Carson Duke was feeling, thinking. The big decision had been made. The divorce was in play. Now he was feeling a mixture of relief and sorrow and wondering if he was doing the right thing.

Oh, sure, there were plenty of people who divorced with joy in their hearts and a spring in their steps. But they weren't the rule. Generally, people felt the pain of losing something they'd once pinned their hopes and dreams on. Hell, Reed had seen it in his own family time and again. Each of his parents invariably entered a marriage thinking that *this* time would be the last. The *one*. True love and they would finally live happily ever after.

"And they're never right," he murmured, shaking his head.

Once again, he was reminded that he'd made the right life choice in *never* letting himself fall into the trap of convincing himself that good, healthy lust was some kind of romantic love destined to transform his life.

At that thought, he snorted in amusement, then walked back to his desk to begin drafting Carson Duke's divorce papers.

Lilah Strong took her time driving along Pacific Coast Highway. The scenery was wildly different from what she was used to and she intended to enjoy it in spite of the hot ball of anger nestled deep in her belly. She didn't like being angry. It always felt to her like a waste of emotion. The person she was furious with didn't care how she felt. Her anger affected no one but *her*... by making her a little nauseous.

But knowing that did nothing to ease the underlying tension that burned inside her. So rather than try to ease that uncomfortable feeling, she briefly distracted herself by glancing out at the ocean.

It was lovely—surfers gliding toward shore on the

tops of waves. Sunlight glinting off the deep blue surface of the sea. Boats with jewel-toned sails and children
building castles in the sand armed with nothing more
than tiny buckets and shovels.

Lilah was a mountain girl, through and through.
Her preferred view was of a tree-laden slope, wide-
open meadows covered in bright splashes of wildflowers or the snowy mountainsides that backed up to her
house. But looking out at the Pacific was a nice change.
Of course, she had time to look at the sea while driving only because she wasn't actually "driving." It was
more…parking.

Pacific Coast Highway was completely backed up
with locals, tourists and, it seemed to her, every surfer
in Southern California. It was the middle of June and
Lilah could imagine that the crowds would only be getting thicker as the summer went on. But thankfully, that
wouldn't be her problem.

In a day or two, she'd be back in the mountains, leaving her companion here in Orange County. That thought
gave her heart a hard squeeze, but there was nothing she
could do about it. It wasn't as if she'd had a choice in
any of this. If she'd been someone else, maybe she would
have considered ignoring facts. But she couldn't live a
lie. She had to do the right thing—even if it felt wrong.

Glancing into the rearview mirror, she looked at her
companion and said, "You're awfully quiet. Too much
to think about to leave room for talking, hmm? I know
how you feel."

Her own mind was spinning. Lilah had been dread-
ing this trip to California for two weeks and now that
it was here, she was still trying to think of a way out
of the situation she found herself in. But no matter how

she looked at it, Lilah was stuck. As was her friend in the backseat.

If she were doing this on her turf, so to speak, she might feel a little more in control. Back in her small mountain town in Utah, she had friends. People she could count on to stand with her. Here, all she had were her own two feet and that sinking sensation in the pit of her stomach.

Orange County, California, was only an hour-and-a-half flight from Lilah's home, but it might as well have been on the other side of the world. She was walking into the unknown with no way out but *through*.

By the time she parked, helped her friend out of the car and walked into the law office, Lilah's stomach was swirling with nerves. The building was Victorian on the outside and a sweep of glass and chrome on the inside. It was unsettling, as if designed to keep clients off guard, and maybe that was the idea. The floors were a polished, high-gleam hardwood, but the walls were decorated with modern paintings consisting of splashes of bright color. The reception desk where a stern-faced, middle-aged woman sat sentry was a slab of glass atop shining steel legs. Even the banister gliding along the wood staircase was made up of steel spindles faced with a wall of glass. It was cold, sterile and just a little intimidating. Oh, she was now sincerely prepared to dislike the man she was there to see. Lilah stiffened her spine and approached the reception desk. "I'm Lilah Strong. I'm here to see Reed Hudson."

The woman looked from Lilah to her friend and back again. "Do you have an appointment?"

"No. I'm here on behalf of his sister, Spring Hudson

Bates," Lilah said and watched a flicker of interest glitter in the woman's eyes. "It's important that I see him now."

"One moment." The woman watched Lilah as she picked up a phone and pressed a single button. "Mr. Hudson, there's a woman here to see you. She claims to have been sent by your sister Spring."

*Claims?* Lilah swallowed the spurt of impatience that jumped into her throat. It took another moment or two before the receptionist hung up and waved one hand at the staircase. "Mr. Hudson will see you. Up the stairs, first door on the left."

"Thank you." Lilah and her companion walked away, but as she went, she felt the other woman's curious gaze follow her.

At the landing, Lilah paused to settle herself outside the heavy double doors. She took a breath, then turned the knob and walked inside.

The outer office was small, but bright, with sunlight pouring through windows that overlooked the ocean. Lilah stepped inside and took a breath, pausing long enough to appreciate the elegant furnishings. The wood floors shone. In one corner, there was a healthy ficus tree in a silver pot. A pair of gray chairs separated by a black table sat against one wall.

A young woman with short black hair and brown eyes sat at a sleek black desk and gave Lilah a friendly smile as she entered. "Hello. I'm Karen, Mr. Hudson's executive assistant. You must be Ms. Strong. Mr. Hudson's waiting for you."

She stood and walked to a pair of double doors. Opening them, she stepped back and Lilah steeled herself before she walked into the lion's den.

The man's office was enormous—no doubt designed

to impress and intimidate. *Mission accomplished*, she thought. A wall of glass behind his desk afforded a spectacular view of the ocean, and on her left, the glass wall continued, displaying a bird's-eye view of Pacific Coast Highway and the crowds that cluttered the street and sidewalks.

The wood floor shone here, too, with the slices of sunlight lying on it sparkling like diamonds. There were several expensive-looking rugs dotting the floor, and the furniture here was less chrome and more dark leather. Still didn't seem to fit in a Victorian building, but it was less startling to the senses than the first-floor decor. But, Lilah told herself, she wasn't here to critique the results of what some designer had done to the stately old building. Instead, she was here to face down the man now standing up behind his desk.

"Who are you?" he demanded. "And what do you know about my sister Spring?"

His voice was deep, rumbling around the room like thunder. He was tall—easily six feet three or four—with thick black hair expensively trimmed to look casual. He wore a black, pin-striped suit and a white dress shirt accented with a red power tie. His shoulders were broad, his jaw square, his eyes green, and as they focused on her, they didn't look friendly.

Well, she thought, that was fine, since she wasn't feeling very friendly, either. He was as intimidating as the plush office, and far more attractive—which had nothing to do with anything, she reminded herself.

Still, she was glad she'd taken care with her appearance before this meeting. At home, she went days without even bothering with makeup. Today, she wore her own version of a power suit. Black slacks, red shirt and short red jacket. Her black boots had a two-inch heel, adding to her five-foot-six-inch height. She was as prepared for this meeting as it was possible to be. Which wasn't saying much.

"I'm Lilah Strong."

"I was told who you are," he said. "What I don't know is why you're here."

"Right." She took a deep breath, then blew it out again. Deliberately striding across the floor in a quick march, she heard her heels click on the wood then soften on the rugs as she approached him. When she was so close she caught a whiff of his aftershave—a subtle scent that reminded her of the forests at home—she stopped. With his wide, black matte desk between them, she looked into his deep green eyes and said, "Spring was my friend. That's why I'm here. She asked me to do something for her and I couldn't say no. That's the *only* reason I'm here."

"All right."

That deep voice seemed to reverberate inside her, leaving her more shaken than she wanted to admit. Why was he so gorgeous? Why did the wary look in his eyes seem sexy rather than irritating? And *why* was she letting an unwanted attraction scatter her thoughts?

"I'm curious." His gaze flicked briefly to Lilah's friend before shifting back to her. "Do you usually bring your baby with you to meetings?"

She lifted her chin and glanced down at the baby girl on her left hip. Here was the reason for leaving home, for facing down a man with ice in his eyes. If it had been up to her, Lilah never would have come. She wouldn't be standing here in Reed Hudson's office with a ball of cold lead in the pit of her stomach. But this wasn't her choice and no matter how hard it was, she would do as Spring had asked.

Rosie slapped both hands together and squealed. Lilah's answering smile faded as she turned her gaze back to the man watching her.

"Rose isn't my baby," she said, with more than a twinge of regret as she met his gaze coolly. "She's *yours*."

# Two

Instantly, Reed went on red alert.

The cold, dispassionate demeanor that had made him a legend in court dropped over him like a familiar jacket. The woman looking at him as if he were a worm, just slithering out from under a rock, was beautiful but clearly delusional.

Over the years, there had been a few predatory women who'd tried to convince him they were pregnant with his child. But, since he was always careful, he'd been able to get rid of them easily enough. And this woman, he'd never been with. That he was sure of, since a man didn't forget a woman like this one.

"I don't have a baby." The very idea was ludicrous. Given his background, his family, his career, if there was one lesson he'd learned it was don't build a family of his own. Since he was sixteen, he'd never been without a condom. "If that's all," he continued briskly, "you can show yourself out."

"Nice," she commented with a slow shake of her head.

The tone of her voice caught his attention. It was just as coolly dismissive as his own. His gaze caught hers and he couldn't mistake the anger and disdain shining in those clear blue eyes. "Problem?"

"No more than I expected from a man like you," she countered and bounced a little, as if to entertain the baby babbling on her hip.

"A man like me," he repeated, curious now. "And you know me, *how*?"

"I know that you were Spring's brother and that you weren't there to help her when she needed it." Her words rushed out as if flowing on a tide of fury. "I know that when you see a child who looks just like your sister you don't even ask a question."

His eyes narrowed. "My sister."

She huffed out a breath. "That's what I said." Briefly, she looked at the baby and her mouth curved slightly. "Her name is Rose and she's Spring's daughter." At the mention of her name, the tiny girl bounced in place and slapped her hands against the woman's shoulder. "That's right, Rosie. You're your mommy's girl, aren't you?"

As if in answer, the baby clapped tiny hands and chortled in some weird baby version of a giggle. And while the two of them smiled at each other, Reed shifted his gaze from the lovely woman to the baby in her arms. *Spring's daughter.* Now that he knew, now that he wasn't on automatic defense, he could see his sister's features, miniaturized on her child. Fine, black hair curling about

a rounded face. Eyes so green they shone like emeralds—
the same shade as Spring's.

As his own, come to that.

Instantly, without even being told, he *knew* his sister
was gone. Spring had looked all her life for real love.
There wasn't a chance in hell she ever would have left
her daughter if she'd had a choice.

And the baby was clearly a Hudson. Then there was
the fact that even in so small a child, he saw the stubborn chin his sister had boasted. Spring had a daughter
he'd known nothing about. He understood the woman's
anger now. Her accusation of not being there for Spring
when she needed him most. But he would have been,
he assured himself silently. If she'd come to him, he'd
have—how was it possible that she *hadn't* come to him?
*Everyone* in his family came to him for help. Why hadn't
Spring?

Then he remembered the last time he saw his younger
sister. More than two years ago, Spring had come to
him, wanting him to arrange for an advance on her trust.
She'd been in love. Again.

Frowning, he remembered his reaction, too. Spring
was one of those people who went through life wearing rose-colored glasses. She saw only the best in people—even those who had no best at all. Spring refused
to recognize that *some* people simply weren't worth her
loyalty or her affection.

It had been the third time she'd been in love—and
that last time was just like the others before had been.
Without fail, Spring seemed to migrate toward men with
few morals, little ambition and less money. He'd always
thought it was because Spring thought she could "save"
them. And that never worked.

Always on the lookout for love, she would invariably end up in Reed's office asking for money to pay off the latest loser so she could move on with her life. But that last time, Reed had been forewarned by yet another sister. Savannah had met Spring's lover and she'd been worried enough that she'd called Reed. He'd run a background check on Spring's love of the moment and found a criminal background—fraud, identity theft and forgery. But Spring hadn't wanted to hear the warnings. She had insisted that Coleman Bates had changed. That he deserved a second chance.

Reed recalled clearly telling her that the man had *had* a second chance—even a third—and hadn't changed. But Spring was in love and wouldn't listen. Standing there now, though, in front of the child she'd left behind, Reed frowned, remembering he'd told Spring to grow the hell up and stop expecting him to sweep in and take care of whatever mess she created. Hurt, angry, Spring had walked out of his office. So later, when she'd really needed him, his sister hadn't called on Reed. And now it was too late for him to make it up to her.

A swift stab of guilt pierced the edges of Reed's heart but he fought it back. Regret was indulgence. It wouldn't help Spring, couldn't ease the pain of her loss. He'd done what he thought was best for his sister at the time. For the family. And if she had come to him for help in extricating herself from the relationship, he assured himself, he would have done all he could for her. Now all he could do was find answers.

"What happened to Spring?"

"She died two months ago."

He gritted his teeth as the harsh truth shook him to his bones. He'd known it, *felt* it, but somehow hearing it made it harder. A quick, sharp slash of pain tore at him and was immediately buried beneath a fresh wave of regret, sorrow. Reed scrubbed one hand across his face then focused on the baby again before shifting to meet Lilah Strong's clear blue eyes. "That's hard to hear."

Spring was his half sister on his father's side and five years younger than Reed. She'd always been so bright, so happy, so damn trusting. And now she was gone.

"I'm sorry. I shouldn't have said it so abruptly."

Shaking his head, he stared into those eyes of hers. So blue, they were nearly violet. They shone with sympathy he didn't want and didn't need. His pain was private. Not something he would share with anyone, let alone a stranger.

To cover the turmoil raging within, he said simply, "There is no way to soften news like that."

"You're right. Of course, you're right." Those eyes shifted, changed with her emotions, and now he read grief of her own mingling with a simmering anger in their depths.

He was no more interested in that than he was in her sympathy.

"What happened to my sister?"

"There was a car accident," she said simply. "Someone ran a red light…"

His eyes narrowed. "Drunk driver?"

"No," she said, shaking her head and patting the baby's back all at once. "An elderly man had a heart attack. He was killed in the accident, as well."

So there was no one to hold responsible. No one to be furious with. To blame. Reed was left with an impotent feeling that he didn't care for.

"You said this happened two months ago," he said

quietly, thoughtfully. "Why are you only coming to me now?"

"Because I didn't know about you," she said, then looked around the office. "Look, the baby needs a change. Do you mind if we take this conversation over to the couch?"

"What?"

She was already headed for his black leather sofa. Before he could say anything, she'd set the infant down and reached into what had to be a diaper bag slung over her shoulder for supplies.

Struck dumb by the action, he only watched as she expertly changed the baby's diaper, then handed the folded-up used one to him. "What am I supposed to do with this?"

Reluctantly, it seemed, her mouth curved and damned if he didn't like the look of it.

"Um," she said wryly, "I'd go for throwing it away."

Stupid. Of course. He glanced at his small office trash can, then shook his head, crossed to the door and opened it. Signaling to his assistant, he held out the diaper and ordered, "Dispose of this."

"Yes, sir." Karen accepted the diaper as she would have an explosive device, then turned away.

Once the door was closed again, Reed looked at the baby, now standing alongside the glossy black coffee table, smacking both hands on the surface and laughing to herself. Shaking his head, he thought of Spring and felt another quick twinge of pain. Still watching the baby, he asked Lilah, "What did you mean you didn't know about me until now?"

She tossed that thick mass of wavy red-gold hair behind her shoulder and looked up at him as she repacked the baby's supplies. "I mean, that until last week, I didn't know Spring had a family. She never talked about you. About any relatives at all. I thought she was alone."

That stung more than he would have thought possible. His sister had wiped him from her life? So much so that her best friend didn't even know of his existence? He scrubbed one hand across his face and regretted that last conversation with his sister. Maybe he could have been kinder. More understanding. But he'd assumed, as he supposed everyone did, that there would be more time. That he would, once again, be called on to dig Spring out of trouble, and so he'd been impatient and now she was gone and the chance to make things right had vanished with her.

"She left two letters," Lilah said and held out an envelope toward him. "I read mine. This one is yours."

Reed took it, checked that it was still sealed, then noted Spring's familiar scrawl across the front. He glanced at the baby, still entertaining herself, then he opened the envelope and pulled out the single sheet of paper.

*Reed. If you're reading this, I'm dead. God, that's a weird thought. But if Lilah brought you this letter, she's also brought you my daughter. I'm asking you to take care of her. Love her. Raise her. Yes, I know I could ask Mom or one of my sisters, but honestly, you're the only one in our family I can really count on.*

Well, that hit him hard, considering that in their last conversation he hadn't given her the help she'd wanted. Gritting his teeth, he went back to the letter.

*Rosie needs you, Reed. I'm trusting you to do the right thing because you always do. Lilah Strong has been my friend and my family for almost two years, so play nice. She's also been Rosie's "other mother," so she can answer any questions you have and she can be a big help to you.*

*As usual, you were right about Coleman. He left as soon as I got pregnant. But before he left, I got him to sign away his rights to Rosie. She doesn't need him in her life.*

*I love you, Reed, and I know Rosie will, too. So thanks in advance—or from the grave. Whichever. Spring.*

He didn't know whether to smile or howl. The letter was so like Spring—making light of a situation that most people wouldn't think about. In seconds, vignettes of Spring's life raced through Reed's mind. He saw her as a baby, a child who followed him around whenever they were together, a teenager who loved nothing more than shocking her parents and finally, a woman who never found the kind of love she'd always searched for.

He folded the paper slowly, then tucked it away again before he let himself look at Spring's child. The baby was clearly well cared for, loved…happy.

Now it was up to him to see that she stayed that way. At that thought everything in Reed went cold and still. He knew what his duty was. Knew what Spring would expect of him. But damned if he knew a thing about babies.

"I see panic in your eyes."

Instantly, Reed's normal demeanor dropped over him. He sent Lilah a cool stare. "I don't panic."

"Really?" she said, clearly not believing him. "Because your expression tells me you're wishing Rosie and I were anywhere but here."

He didn't appreciate being read so easily. Reed had been told by colleagues and judges alike that his poker face was the best in the business. Knowing one small baby and one very beautiful woman had shattered his record was a little humbling. But no need to let her know that.

"You're wrong. What I'm wondering is what I'm going to do next." And that didn't come easy to him, either. Reed always had a plan. And a backup plan. And a plan to use if the backup failed. But at the moment, he was at a loss.

"What you're going to do?" The woman stood up, smiled down at the baby then turned a stony stare on him. "You're going to take care of Rosie."

"Obviously," he countered. The question was, *how*? Irritated, he pushed one hand through his hair and muttered, "I'm not exactly prepared for a baby."

"No one ever is," Lilah told him. "Not even people who like to plan their lives down to the last minute. Babies throw every plan out the nearest window."

"Wonderful."

Rosie squealed until the sound hit a pitch Reed was afraid might make his ears bleed. "That can't be normal."

Lilah laughed. "She's a happy baby."

Tipping her head to one side, Lilah watched him. "After I found out about Spring's family, I did some research. I know you have a lot of siblings, so you must be used to babies."

Another irritation, that he'd been looked into, though

he knew potential clients did it all the time. "Yeah, a lot of siblings that I usually saw once or twice a year."

"Not a close family," she mused.

"You could say that," Reed agreed. Hard to be close, though, when there were so damn many of them. You practically needed a spreadsheet just to keep track of his relatives.

"My family's not at issue right now," he said, shifting his gaze away from blue eyes trying to see too much to the baby looking up at him with Spring's eyes. "Right now, I've got a problem to solve."

Lilah sighed. "She's not a problem, she's a *baby*."

Reed flicked Lilah a glance. "She's also my problem. Now."

He would take care of her, raise her, just as his sister had wanted. But first, he had to get things lined up. He'd made his fortune, survived his wildly eclectic family, by having a plan and sticking to it. The plan now entailed arranging for help in taking care of Spring's daughter.

He worked long hours and would need someone on site to handle the child's day-to-day needs. It would take a little time to arrange for the best possible nanny. So the problem became what to do with the baby until he could find the right person.

His gaze settled on Lilah Strong. And he considered the situation. She already knew and cared about the baby. Yes, she still looked as though she'd like to slap him, but that didn't really matter, did it? What was important was getting the baby settled in. He had a feeling he could convince this woman to help him with that. If he offered her enough money to compensate her for her time.

He knew better than most just how loudly money

could talk to those who didn't have any. "I have a proposition for you."

Surprise, then suspicion, flashed in her blue eyes just before they narrowed on him. "What sort of proposition?"

"The sort that involves a lot of money," he said shortly, then turned and walked to his desk. Reaching into the bottom drawer, he pulled out a leather-bound checkbook and laid it, open and ready, on top of his desk. "I want to hire you to stay for a while. Take care of the baby—"

"Her *name* is Rosie..."

"Right. Take care of Rosie then, until I can arrange for a full-time nanny." He picked up a pen, clicked it into life then gave her a long, cool look. "I'll pay whatever you want."

Her mouth dropped open and she laughed shortly, shaking her head as if she couldn't believe what was happening. Fine. If she was unable to come up with a demand, he'd make an offer and they could negotiate from there. "Fifty thousand dollars," he said easily.

"Fifty?" Her eyes were wide. Astonished.

"Not enough? All right, a hundred thousand." Normally, he might have bid lower, but this was an emergency and he couldn't afford to have her say no.

"Are you crazy?"

"Not at all," he said with a shrug to emphasize that the money meant nothing to him. "I pay for what I need when I need it. And, as I believe it will take me at least a week or two to find and hire an appropriate nanny, I'm willing to buy interim help."

"I'm not for sale."

He smiled now. How many times had he heard that

statement just before settling on the right amount? Everyone had a price—the only challenge came in finding the magic number. "I'm not trying to buy you," Reed assured her, "just rent you for a week or two."

"You have enough arrogance for two or three people," she said.

He straightened up, shot her a level look. "It's not arrogance. It's doing what needs to be done. I can do that with your help—which allows you to continue to be a part of the child's—"

"Rosie's—"

"—life," he finished with a nod at her correction. "You can stay, make sure the person I hire is right for the job. Or, you can leave and go home now."

Of course, he didn't believe for a moment that she would leave the baby until she was absolutely sure of the child's well-being. That was written all over her face. Her body language practically *screamed* defensive mode. And he would use her desire to protect the baby for his own purposes. Reed Hudson always got what he wanted. Right now, that included Lilah Strong.

He could see her thinking and it wasn't difficult to discern her thoughts from the expressions flitting across her features. She was still furious with him for whatever reasons, but she wasn't ready to walk away from the baby yet. She would need to see for herself that Rosie was settled into her new home.

So, whether she realized it or not, Lilah Strong would do exactly what Reed wanted.

"I'll stay," she said finally, still watching the baby stagger around the coffee table like a happy drunk. "Until you've found the right nanny."

Then she turned and looked at Reed. "But I won't be paid. I won't be *rented*. I'll do it for Rosie. Not you."

He hid a smile. "Good. Now, I've a few more appointments this afternoon, so why don't you and the—" he caught himself and said instead "—*Rosie* head over to my place. I'll be there at about six."

"Fine," she said. "Where do you live?"

"My assistant, Karen, will give you all of the particulars." He checked the platinum watch on his wrist. "For now…"

"Fine. You're busy. I get it." She slung the diaper bag over her shoulder, then reached down to scoop up the baby. Once Rosie was settled on her hip, she looked up at him. "I'll see you later then. We can talk about all of this."

"All right." He kept the satisfaction he felt out of his voice. She walked past him and her scent seemed to reach out for him. Lemons, he thought. Lemons and sage. It was every bit as tantalizing as the woman herself.

He watched her go, his gaze sliding from the lush fall of that golden red hair down to the curve of a first-class behind. His body stirred as her scent seemed to sink deep inside him, making him want things that would only complicate an already messy situation.

Knowing that, though, didn't ease the hunger.


"You *live* in a hotel?" Lilah demanded the moment Reed walked through the door later that afternoon.

For hours, she'd wandered the expansive suite, astonished at the luxury, the oddity, of anyone actually living in a hotel. Okay, her own mother and stepfather lived on board a cruise ship, traveling constantly from country to country. They enjoyed being somewhere different every day, though it would have driven Lilah crazy.

But living in a hotel? When there were a zillion houses to choose from? Who did that? Well, all right, she'd heard of movie stars doing it, but Reed Hudson was a lawyer, for heaven's sake. Granted, a very successful, obviously very *rich* lawyer, but still. Didn't the man want a home? A hotel was so…impersonal.

Though she'd noticed a lot of framed photos of what had to be members of his family scattered throughout the two-bedroom, two-bath suite. So, she told herself, he wasn't as separate from the Hudson clan as he pretended. That made her feel both better and worse.

Better because Rosie would have more family than just this one seemingly cold and distant man. But worse because if he did care about his family, why hadn't he been there for Spring when she'd needed him?

He shut the door behind him, then simply stood there, staring at her. Those green eyes of his seemed to spear right through her and Lilah could only imagine how good he must be in court. Any opposing witness would quail beneath that steady, cool stare.

"You have a problem with the hotel suite?" He tucked both hands into the pockets of his slacks.

"It's lovely and you know it." And, unlike his office, the space was decorated in more than black, chrome and gray.

The living room was wide and dotted with twin lemon-yellow chairs opposite a sky blue sofa, all of them overstuffed and just begging someone to drop in and relax for a while. The tables were a honey-colored wood and the rugs on the tile floor were splashes of jewel tones. There was an oak dining set at the edge of a

small, stocked wet bar, and a grouping of cream-colored
lounge chairs on the terrace ran the length of the suite.
Each of the two bedrooms was done in shades of cream
and green and the bathrooms were luxurious, spa-like
spaces with stand-alone tubs big enough to hold a party
in and showers studded with full-body sprays.

From the terrace, there was a spectacular view of the
ocean in the distance, with the meticulously cared-for
golf course and a sea of red-tiled roofs in the surround-
ing neighborhood closer up. The hotel itself looked like
a castle plunked down in the middle of a beach city and
felt light-years away from her own home, a cabin in the
mountains.

Though it was much smaller than this hotel suite, her
cabin afforded beautiful views, too, of a lake and the
mountains and a meadow that in spring was dotted with
wildflowers and the deer that came to graze through it.
She was out of her element here and that made her feel
slightly off balance. Which, Lilah told herself, was not a
good thing when dealing with a man like Reed Hudson.

"Where's the baby?" he asked, his gaze shifting
around the room before settling on her again.

*"Rosie—"* she emphasized the baby girl's name "—
is asleep in the crib the hotel provided." Honestly, how
was he going to be a parent to the little girl if he couldn't
even seem to say her name?

"Good." He slipped out of his jacket, tossed it across
the back of a chair and walked toward the wet bar near
the gas fireplace. As he reached for a bottle of scotch,
he loosened the precise knot of his tie and opened the
collar of his shirt. Why that minor action should strike
Lilah as completely sexy, she couldn't have said.

"I called ahead," Reed was saying. "Told Andre you

were coming and to see that you had everything you needed."

"Andre." Lilah thought back to the moment she'd entered the hotel to be greeted by an actual *butler*. If it hadn't been for the man's friendly smile and eagerness to help, she might have been completely intimidated by the snooty accent and his quiet efficiency. "He was wonderful. Couldn't do enough to help us and Rosie loved him. But I can't believe this suite comes with a butler."

One corner of his mouth quirked as he poured himself a scotch. "Andre's more than a butler. Sometimes I think he's a miracle worker."

"I'm convinced," she admitted. "He arranged for the crib and had a wide selection of baby food stocked in your pantry. He even provided a bright blue teddy bear that Rosie already loves."

Reed smiled and even from across the room Lilah felt the punch of it. If anything, her sense of balance dissolved just a bit more.

"You want a drink?"

She thought about refusing, simply because she wasn't ready to relax around him yet. But after the day she'd had… "Wine, if you have it. White."

He nodded, got the wine from the refrigerator and poured her a glass. Carrying both drinks to the sofa, he sat down and handed the wine to her when she joined him, taking a seat on the opposite corner.

Lilah took a sip, let the wine settle her a bit. Being this close to Reed Hudson was a little unnerving. The anger she'd been living with for the past few weeks still simmered deep inside her, but looking at him now, she had to admit it wasn't only anger she was feeling. She had another slow sip of wine and reminded herself just why she was there.

"Why are you so willing to raise Rosie?" she asked, her voice shattering the silence.

He studied the golden scotch in the heavy glass tumbler for a long moment before taking a swallow. "Because Spring asked me to."

"Just like that."

He looked at her, his green eyes as clear and sharp as emeralds under a spotlight. "Just like that. The baby— *Rosie*—" he corrected before she could "—is a Hudson. She's family and I look out for my family."

"Enough to change your whole life?"

A wry smile curved his mouth briefly. "Life's always changing," he mused. "With a family like mine, nothing ever stays the same."

"Okay, but…" Waving one hand to encompass the elegant surroundings, Lilah said, "You're not exactly living in a baby-friendly environment."

"I know." His gaze slipped around the open room, then he nodded at her. "That's one of the reasons you're here. You've got more experience with babies than I do. So you'll know how to baby-proof this place temporarily."

"Temporarily?" she asked.

"Obviously, I'll need a house," he said, taking another drink of his scotch. "Until now, the hotel's worked well for me. Butler service, daily maids and twenty-four-hour room service."

"It does sound good," she admitted, but didn't think she'd be able to live in such a cutoff, sterile environment for long.

"But a baby changes things," he added, with a slight frown into his glass.

"Yeah, they really do."

Abruptly, he pushed to his feet and reached out for her hand.

"What?" she asked.

One eyebrow winged up. "Don't be so suspicious. Just come with me for a minute."

She placed her hand in his and completely ignored the buzz of something electric that zapped through her. If he felt it, too, he was much better at not showing it than she was. Not a flicker of response shone in his eyes as he pulled her to her feet.

He tugged her behind him as he walked around the sofa, across the room and out onto the terrace, stepping into the encroaching shadows. Then he let her go and walked up to the stone railing, looking out over the view as lights began to wink into existence in the homes below, and a handful of stars began to glitter in the sky.

Lilah followed his gaze briefly, then half turned to watch him instead. His sharp green eyes were narrowed against the cold wind that ruffled his thick, wavy black hair. Somehow he seemed more…approachable. Which should probably worry her.

"I can't stay here," he said, his voice soft enough that she leaned in closer so she wouldn't miss a word. "Rosie will need a yard. And a terrace that doesn't include a couple-hundred-foot drop to the street."

Lilah shivered and looked over the edge of the railing. She'd had the same hideous thought herself. A tiny Rosie crawling out to the terrace and somehow climbing up on furniture and pitching right over. Deliberately, she pushed that mental image away and told herself it was good that Reed had come to the decision to move on his own—without her having to mention it.

"So just like that, you'll buy a house."

"Just like that," he assured her, turning to lean one hip against the stone balustrade. "I'll find something this weekend."

She laughed. How could she not? Lilah's friends worked and saved for months, sometimes years to sock away enough money to maybe look for a house. Reed Hudson would simply pull out his magic checkbook. "Is everything so easy then?"

"Not easy," he assured her, his green eyes meeting and holding hers. "But if there's one thing I know—it's that if you want something, you go get it."

# Three

Oddly enough, Lilah could understand that statement. Okay, the spur-of-the-moment buying of a house was way out of her league, but the *attitude* was something she believed in. Going after what you wanted and not giving up until you had it.

Isn't that how she'd run her own life?

How strange that she found herself agreeing with a man she'd expected to loathe on general principle. But as much as she was still furious on her friend's behalf, she had to admit that Spring had left her daughter to Reed's care. That said something, too, didn't it?

Spring had loved her daughter more than anything. So Lilah had to assume that there was more to Reed Hudson than she'd seen so far. Rose would not have been entrusted to him if Spring hadn't believed he could and would love that little girl.

Maybe, Lilah thought, instead of just holding her own anger close and nurturing it, she should give him a chance to show her she was wrong about him.

"How does Rosie fit into your plans?" she asked.

He looked at her for a long minute and Lilah just managed to keep from fidgeting beneath that steady stare. Her hormones were stirring to life, and that was so unexpected. She'd come here reluctantly, to turn over a baby she loved to a man she didn't know or trust. Now her own body was lighting up in a way she'd never known before, and she didn't like it. Being attracted to this man wasn't something she wanted—but her body didn't seem to care.

Under the gaze from hot green eyes, she shifted uncomfortably and silently told herself to get a grip.

"Rosie's mine now." Cool words uttered simply and they drove a knife through her heart.

Instantly, she told herself that she should be glad of it. That's why she was here, after all. But she'd loved Rose from the moment of her birth. Lilah was Spring's coach all through labor and delivery and she'd held Rosie herself when the little girl was moments old. She had been a part of the baby's life from that day on, helping to care for her, worrying about her, *loving* her. And since Spring's death more than a month ago, Lilah and Rosie had been a team. A unit. Now she had to give up the child she loved so much and it tore at her.

"I'll take care of her," he was saying. "Just as Spring wanted me to."

"Good," she muttered, and paused for a sip of wine. "That's good."

"Yes," he said wryly. "I can hear just how pleased you are about it."

Caught, she shrugged. "No point in pretending, is there?"

"None." He nodded. "Truth is much easier and far less trouble."

"Are you sure you're a lawyer?"

One eyebrow winged up. "Don't much like lawyers?"

"Does anyone?"

His mouth twitched briefly. "Good point. Though I can say my clients end up very fond of me."

"I'll bet," Lilah muttered. In all of her research, she'd learned just what a shark Reed Hudson was in a court-room. He was right, his clients did love him, but, oh, his opponents had plenty to say—most of it sour grapes, but still.

Frowning, he gave her a hard, long look and asked, "So is it lawyers you loathe or just *me* in particular?"

"I don't know you well enough to loathe you," she admitted, which wasn't really answering the question. She gave a sigh, met his gaze and said, "I came here already not liking you much."

"Yes, that was clear when we met."

Lilah winced a little. She was never deliberately rude, but her emotions had nearly been choking her. It wasn't really an excuse, but it was the only one she had. "You're right. But losing Spring, then having to hand Rosie over to someone I'd never met…"

She watched him think, consider, before he finally nodded. "I can see that," he acknowledged with another long look into her eyes. "I appreciate loyalty."

"So do I," she said and thought they'd finally found some common ground.

"I spoke to our parents," he said abruptly. "Well," he amended, "our father, Spring's mother."

So strange, Lilah thought, different parents, same family, tangled and twisted threads of connections. Lilah had had no idea that Spring was a member of such a well-known family. Until her death revealed her secrets, Spring had gone by her ex-husband's last name, Bates. So Lilah hadn't been at all prepared to face down the powerful Hudson family.

Worry tightened into a coil in the pit of her stomach. What if Spring's parents wanted Rosie? Would he give the baby over, in spite of Spring's request that he raise her? And if he wanted to, how could Lilah fight him on it? From what she'd learned about the Hudsons, she had to think their parents were less than interested in their own children. They wouldn't give Rosie the time or care she needed. Even while a part of her started plotting just what she might do if she had to take on Spring's parents, Lilah asked, "What did they say?"

He sighed and for the first time he looked more tired than irritated. Or maybe, she thought, *resigned* was the right word.

"Just what I expected them to say," he told her with a wry twist to his lips. "My father reminded me that he already has a three-year-old in the house and his wife is about to give birth to another baby."

She blinked. It sounded strange to hear about siblings born more than thirty years apart.

"And Spring's mother, Donna, said she's got no interest in being a grandmother—or in having anyone find out she's old enough to *be* a grandmother."

"Not very maternal, is she?"

"The words *alley cat* spring to mind," he admitted. "My father has interesting taste in women. Anyway, I told them both that Spring left her child to me. I was only calling them to give them a heads-up."

A quiet sigh of relief slid from Lilah's lungs. He didn't sound as though he had any interest in handing Rosie over to those people, so one worry down. "So basically," she said through the quiet sigh of relief, "they're leaving Rosie with you."

He looked at her. "I wouldn't have given Rose to them even if they'd wanted her—which I was certain they wouldn't."

Now surprise flickered to life inside her. Lilah would have expected him to *want* someone to relieve him of the baby. Hearing him say just the opposite made her wonder about him. "Why?"

Frowning, he took a drink, then said, "First and most importantly, Spring asked me to take care of her daughter."

Lilah nodded. She understood and appreciated that he would take his sister's request to heart. In everything she'd read about him, he was a cold, merciless attorney. What she hadn't known about was the loyalty she saw now, etched into his expression.

And even though her heart ached at the thought of going home and leaving Rosie behind... Lilah felt a bit better about going knowing that at least Reed would do what his own sense of duty demanded. It wasn't enough for a child to grow on. A child needed love before anything else. But it was a start.

Still, she asked, "What else? What aren't you saying?"

His mouth firmed into a tight line as he shifted his gaze from hers to the ocean, where the dying sun layered brilliant streaks of red and gold across the water. "Your parents," he asked, "still together?"

A bittersweet pang of old pain shot through her chest. "They were," she said quietly, watching his profile as he studied the sea as if looking for answers. "Until my father died in an avalanche five years ago."

He looked at her then, briefly. "I'm sorry."

"So were we," she said, remembering that loss and how keenly it had been felt. "A couple of years ago, though, my mother met someone. He's a very nice man and he makes her happy. They were married a year ago, and now they spend all of their time traveling."

Stan was retired, having sold his business for millions more than ten years ago. When he met Lilah's mother on a ski run in Utah, it really had been love at first sight, for both of them. And though it had been hard to accept that her mother could love someone other than Lilah's father, she couldn't deny how happy Stan made her mom.

Curiosity sparked in his eyes. "Going where?"

"Everywhere, really," she said, with a half laugh. "Mom and Stan live on a cruise ship, going from port to port and, according to my mother's emails, having a wonderful time."

Now he turned, a small smile curving his mouth, and looked down at her. "You were surprised that I live in a hotel, but your own mother lives on a cruise ship."

She shrugged. "But a hotel's on land. Near houses. A cruise ship is something else again."

"Odd logic."

Smiling, she said, "It works for me."

"Yeah." He turned his face into the wind again and said, "So, my family's different. They like having children, they just don't like having them around. Nannies, governesses and boarding schools are the favorite child-rearing tools for the Hudsons."

Before she could say anything about that, he went on, "Spring hated it. It was a kind of torture for her to be locked away in a school she couldn't leave." He swiveled his head and stared at her. "How could I give Rose over to people who would only do the same thing to her that they did to her mother? No."

Warmth opened up in the center of her chest and Lilah was caught off guard. The cold, hard lawyer seemed to have disappeared and she didn't know quite what to make of the man he was now.

"You've agreed to stay," he was saying, and Lilah came up out of her thoughts to listen.

"For a while, yes." For Rosie. For Lilah's own sake, she would stay until she was sure the baby girl would be safe. Happy. She'd closed her artisanal soap shop temporarily and could run the online business from her laptop, so there was no rush to get home.

Reed had wanted to *pay* her to stay. What he didn't realize was he would have had to pay her to *leave*.

"Then you can help me choose the house." He finished off his scotch. "And furnish it. I won't have time for a decorator."

Stunned, she just looked at him. "You want me to—"

"Don't all women like shopping?"

She laughed shortly. "That's completely sexist."

"Sue me. Am I wrong?"

"No, but that's not the point," she said.

"It's exactly the point. You'll have free rein," he tempted her. "You can pick out the furnishings that'll make the house baby friendly."

Help choose the kind of house Rosie would grow up in? How could she refuse? Shopping to outfit an entire house on someone else's dime? What woman wouldn't accept that offer? Besides, if left to his own devices, Lilah was sure he'd furnish the whole place in black and white, and that thought was just too hideous to contemplate.

"Free rein?" she repeated, wanting his assurances.

"That's what I said."

"So you're okay with lots of color."

His eyes narrowed. "How much color?"

He was worried and that made her smile. "Free rein," she reminded him.

Buying a house wasn't that difficult when you were willing to pay any price to get what you wanted when you wanted it. The Realtor quickly decided that Lilah was the person she needed to convince, and so Reed was able to hang back and watch the show. He had to admit, Lilah was picky, but she knew what would work and what wouldn't. She wasn't easily swayed by the Realtor's practiced patter about square footage, views and school districts. He admired that.

But then, he was finding the whole package of Lilah Strong intriguing. She wasn't sure of him still, so there was a simmer of anger about her he couldn't miss. Most women he knew were cautious enough to only let him see carefully constructed smiles. They laughed at his jokes, sighed at his kiss and in general tried to make themselves into exactly what he might want.

Strange, then, that the woman who didn't care what he thought of her was the one he found the most intriguing. Hell, watching her move through an empty house, the Realtor hot on her heels, was entertaining. And damned if the view wasn't a good one.

She wore a long-sleeved white button-down shirt with

a sleek black vest over it. Her blue jeans hugged a great behind and an excellent pair of legs, and black boots with a two-inch heel completed the look. Casual elegance. Her reddish-gold hair hung loose to the middle of her back in a cascade of waves that made him want to bury his hands in the thick mass.

But then, he remembered she'd looked damn good the night before, too, wearing only a sky blue nightgown that stopped midthigh.

*He woke up at the sound of the baby crying and realized that this was his new reality. Rose was his now and he took care of what was his.*

*Moving through the darkened suite, he walked to the room Rose and Lilah were sharing, gave a brief knock and opened the door. Lilah was standing in a slice of moonlight, the baby held close to her chest. She was swaying in place and whispering things Reed couldn't make out.*

*"Is she all right?" he asked, keeping his own voice hushed.*

*"Just a little scared," Lilah told him, giving the baby soothing pats as she rocked her gently. "New place."*

*"Right." Wearing only a pair of cotton sleep pants, he walked barefoot across the room and scooped Rose right out of Lilah's arms, cradling the baby to his chest.*

*For a moment, it looked as though Rose would complain. Loudly. But the baby stared at him for a long minute, then sighed and laid her little head down on his shoulder.*

*That one action melted something inside him and felt...powerful. He held that tiny life close, felt her every breath, every shuddering sigh, and knew in that one shining moment he would do anything to keep her safe.*

*Then he looked into Lilah's eyes and found her measuring him. Her hair was a tangle of curls around her face, her eyes were wary and she crossed her arms over her chest, lifting her breasts high enough that he got a glimpse of cleavage at the V-neck of her nightgown.*

*"Sorry she woke you," Lilah said, voice soft as a feather.*

*"I'm not," he said, surprised to find it was nothing but the truth. "We have to get used to each other, don't we?"*

*"Yes, I guess you do." She reached out one hand to smooth her palm over Rosie's dark curls. "She's usually a good sleeper, but her routine's a little messed up right now."*

*"She'll get a new routine soon."*

*At that, Lilah let her hand drop to her side and stared up at him. "Are you ready for that?"*

*He looked down at the baby asleep on his shoulder. "I will be."*

*And in the quiet of the night, with a sleeping baby between them, he and Lilah watched each other in the silence.*

Reed had wondered then, as he did now, if she had felt the heat that snapped and sizzled between them.

Today, her blue eyes were sharp and clear as she inspected the kitchen of the fifth house they'd seen that morning. She stepped out onto a brick patio, with the Realtor hot on her heels. Reed walked out after them, listening to their conversation.

"I like that there's a fence around the pool," Lilah said, looking at it as if she could judge its strength with the power of her gaze.

"Electronic locks with a parental control," the Realtor said, giving a wide, plastic smile as she smoothed black hair so stiff that it probably wouldn't have moved even if she were in the middle of a tornado. "There's a top-of-the-line security system in the house as well, and both remotes are accessible in the garage as well as the house."

"Security," Lilah mused thoughtfully. "So this isn't a good neighborhood?"

The Realtor paled while Reed smothered a smile.

"This is one of the finest neighborhoods in Laguna," the Realtor protested. "A security system is simply for peace of mind."

Reed saw the humor in Lilah's eye and knew she was just giving the other woman a hard time.

"I do like this yard," she said, turning in a slow circle to admire the picture.

Reed did as well, and he had to admit that of the houses they'd seen so far that morning, he preferred this one. The house itself was a larger version of a California bungalow. It had charm, character but plenty of room, and it wasn't sitting on top of its neighbors. He liked that. Reed also liked the yard. The pool took up a third of the lot, but alongside it ran a wide green swath of lawn that would give a kid plenty of room to run. There were trees and flower beds, and since they were situated high on a hill, there were spectacular views of the ocean. The brick terrace boasted an outdoor living space, complete with a backyard kitchen, and the interior of the house was just as perfect. Five bedrooms, five baths and a kitchen that looked fine to him and had had Lilah sighing.

Standing in a tree-dappled patch of shade, Lilah looked at him. "What do you think?"

Both women were watching him, but Reed's gaze met Lilah's alone. "I think it'll work."

The Realtor laughed sharply. "Work? It's a fabulous piece of property. Completely redone two years ago, from the roof to the flooring. It's only been on the market for three days and it's priced to sell and—"

Never taking his gaze from Lilah's, Reed held up one hand for silence and hardly noticed as the Realtor's voice faded away.

Lilah grinned at the woman's reaction to his silent command. "I like it."

"Me, too," Reed said, and spared a glance for the Realtor. "I'll take it. Have the paperwork drawn up and delivered to me at the Monarch this afternoon—"

"This afternoon? I don't know that I can get it all done that quickly and—"

Now he shot the woman a look he generally reserved for hostile witnesses on the stand. "I have every confidence you will. And, while you're working, you should know there's a nice bonus in it for you if you arrange for a seven-day escrow."

"Seven—"

*"And,"* he continued as if she hadn't interrupted, "since I'll be paying cash for the house, I'd like the keys in five days. Furniture has to be delivered and arranged so that we can move in at the end of the seven days."

"That's highly irregular…"

He watched Lilah turn and walk across the yard, as if she'd done her part and didn't feel it necessary to be in on the haggling. Well, he'd rather talk to her, so he wrapped this up quickly.

"Ms. Tyler," he said quietly, firmly, "I doubt you come across many cash clients and so the regular rules may not apply in this situation. Why don't you take care of this and make it happen?"

"I'll do my best, naturally," she blurted, adjusting the fit of her bright red jacket.

"Twenty percent of the asking price as a bonus above your commission."

Her eyes went as wide as the moon and her jaw literally dropped. Not surprising since he was sure she didn't receive that kind of bonus very often. But it was worth it to him.

He didn't like waiting. He didn't mind paying for what he wanted. And Reed knew that money could pave over obstacles faster than anything else in the world. In fact, the only person he'd ever come across who couldn't be bought—or even rented—was Lilah Strong. Just another reason she intrigued him.

He walked past the stunned-into-silence Realtor and moved toward Lilah. Besides, what was the point of being rich if you didn't use the money?

"I'll get right on this," the Realtor called out when she could speak again. "I'll, uh, just wait outside in my car. Start making calls. You and your wife take your time looking around."

He didn't bother to correct the woman, though the word *wife* gave him a quick, cold chill. Instead, he walked slowly across the lawn to join Lilah as she stared out at the view.

"It's done."

She turned. "What?"

"I bought the house."

She laughed and shook her head. The wind lifted her hair and flew it about her face until she reached up and plucked a long strand out of her eyes. "Of course you did. Moving in tonight are you?"

His mouth quirked. "No, I didn't want to rush. Next weekend is soon enough."

Now she laughed and the sound was surprisingly sexy. He moved in closer and caught her scent. Different today, he thought, and realized she now smelled like cinnamon apples. Lemons yesterday, apples today. As if the woman herself wasn't distraction enough.

"You know," she said, "it took me three months to find my house, then it was another month to arrange for a loan, buy it and gain possession and then move in. Most people don't manage it in a week."

"I'm not most people," he said with a shrug.

"That I agree with." She turned, leaned against the chest-high wall and looked at the back of the house. "It is beautiful."

He never took his gaze from her. "It is."

As if feeling him watching her, she turned her head to briefly look at him. The air seemed to sizzle between them. "What're you doing?"

"Just stating the obvious," he said with a half shrug.

She took a deep breath and looked back at the house, ignoring the flash of heat. That irritated. It was there. A hum of something hot, something potent, and she seemed determined to pretend it wasn't.

"Rosie will love having this yard to play in." She sounded wistful. "I'm glad the pool has a fence around it."

"If there hadn't been," he said flatly, "I would have had one installed before we moved in."

She shot him a glance. "In less than a week."

He winked. "Of course."

"Of course." She nodded, sighed. "We should get back to the hotel and check on Rosie."

"She's fine. Andre personally vouched for the hotel babysitter. Apparently she's the grandma type, great with babies."

"I know. He told me."

"But you don't trust anyone but yourself with the baby."

"I didn't say that," she pointed out. "I just don't know her."

"You don't know me, either," Reed said, studying her features. The sun and shadow played across her face, danced in her eyes, highlighting the worry gleaming there. "So how will you handle leaving her with me?"

"Honestly?" She pushed her hair back with a careless swipe of her hand. "I don't know. But, I don't have a choice in that, do I?" She shifted her gaze back to the sea. "I have to do what Spring asked me to, even if I don't like it."

He watched her for a long minute, the set of her chin, her blue eyes narrowed against the glint of the sunlight on the water. Getting back to the hotel, the waiting Realtor out front, left his mind in favor of staying right there, talking to Lilah, finding out more of who and what she was.

"If you hadn't found the letters from Spring, would you have kept Rose yourself?" He already knew the answer, but he wanted to hear her say it.

"Yes," she said firmly. "I'd have adopted her. I would have done anything I had to, to keep her. I already love her like she's my own."

"I noticed," he said, giving her a brief smile when she

looked at him. "It's impressive…letting go of what you want to fulfill Spring's wishes."

"I'm not trying to impress you."

"Another reason why I am impressed," he admitted. "So tell me. How did you and my sister become such good friends?"

Her gaze followed the clouds racing across the sky. A reluctant smile curved her mouth and for a moment or two she seemed lost in her own thoughts, memories. When she spoke, her voice was soft. "She came to my shop, looking for work."

Still having a hard time realizing his sister had had a *job*, Reed chuckled a little at his own memories. "The first and only job Spring had that I know about was at the movie theater the summer she was sixteen." He smiled at the images his mind showed him. "My father had said something about her being unemployable since all she knew how to do was spend his money."

"That was nice," Lilah muttered.

"Yeah, he's a charmer all right. Anyway, Spring decided to prove to our father that she could make her own money." He shook his head, remembering. "She loved movies and thought it would be a great way to see all the new ones when they came out. With the added benefit of making our father eat his words." He sighed a little. "But she worked the candy counter and hardly had the time to see a movie at all. Plus, she hated what she called the 'ugly' uniform. She didn't last a month."

"People change," Lilah said quietly.

"Not in my experience," Reed countered.

"Well, Spring did." Lilah set her hands on top of the wall, rested her chin on them and looked out at the ocean as if looking back in time. "Her husband had just left her. She was pregnant and alone—" she shot him a quick look "—or so I thought. She needed a job and was willing to do anything I needed."

He frowned. "What kind of shop do you own?"

She laughed at the obvious worry in his voice. "It's called Lilah's Bouquet. I sell artisanal soaps and candles."

Did that explain all the different fragrances that seemed to cling to her? Probably.

"And what did Spring do at your shop?"

"Everything." Lilah smiled to herself. "Hiring her was the best decision I ever made, I swear. She was great with customers. Always seemed to know what they'd like and helped them find it. She took care of the stock, kept track of what was selling and what wasn't. Honestly, she was wonderful. Before long, I made her the manager and that gave me more time to spend in my workshop, making up the soaps and candles to stock the shelves."

It was as if she was describing a stranger. Manager? Spring? Frowning, Reed tried to imagine it and came up short. His younger sister had never been the dedicated sort—or at least that's what he'd believed. But it seemed that he hadn't known Spring as a mature adult at all. And now he never would.

"There's a small apartment over the shop," Lilah was saying. "I lived there myself until I could buy a house. So Spring and Rose moved in and it worked well for all of us. The baby charmed every customer who came through the door and Spring didn't have to worry about leaving Rose with a babysitter. Everything was great, until…" Her eyes went dark with grief and memory.

A sharp stab of pain sliced at Reed's heart. He didn't want to think about his sister's death any more than Lilah wanted to talk about it. So instead, he focused on the life she'd been living away from her family. "It sounds like she was happy."

Lilah's gaze lifted to meet his and a sad smile curved her mouth. "She was. She loved our little town and being a part of it. She had a lot of friends."

Reed tried to picture it. His sister, born in London, raised there and in New York. She had gone to the best boarding school in the city and hung out with the children of rock stars and princes. So it was a little hard to picture her happy in a shop apartment in some small town in— "Where?"

"What?"

"Where do you live? Your shop? Your small town? You didn't say."

"You're right. I haven't. There's just been so much going on. It's Pine Lake, Utah. About an hour north of Salt Lake City, up in the Wasatch mountains."

Reed shook his head and chuckled again. "Sorry. Just hard to imagine Spring in the mountains. She was always more for the beach."

"People change."

One dark eyebrow lifted. "Yeah, you've said that before."

She smiled a little. "Must be true then."

"For some people."

She tipped her head to one side and looked up at him through serious eyes. "People can surprise you."

"That's usually the problem," he mused, then took her arm. "We should go. Ms. Tyler's probably sitting out in her car wondering what we're doing back here."

"Right. I want to get back to Rosie, too."

He steered her across the yard and through the open

back door. With his hand at her elbow, they walked through the house that would be his home in a little more than a week, and Reed told himself that sometimes, change happened whether you were ready for it or not.

# Four

The next week was a busy one. She hardly saw Reed, who made himself scarce whenever she and the baby entered a room. He spent most of his time at work and she had to wonder if that situation was normal or if it was simply that he was trying to avoid her completely.

On the other hand, Lilah was really going to miss Andre.

She didn't know what she would have done without him the past several days. Life in a hotel wasn't ideal, but the amazing butler could have made her a believer.

Snooty accent aside, Andre was always ready to help. And though he was loathe to gossip, he had let a few little nuggets of information about Reed drop over the past couple of days. So now she knew that his family rarely visited, he almost never had guests—translation: women—in his suite and that he was a generous tipper.

Which told Lilah that either Reed was a determined loner or he was lonely and that he paid attention when people helped him and made sure to show his appreciation. It wasn't much, but it was more than she'd learned from Reed himself.

Andre cleared his throat to get her attention. "I've prepared another list of furniture shops you might want to check," he said, producing said list from the inside pocket of his immaculate three-piece black suit. Handing it to her, he winked. "I've marked the ones most useful I believe for what you're interested in. As you've already ordered Rose's things, I believe Mr. Hudson's study is the last room on your agenda."

"How do you remember that?" Lilah asked with a laugh. "I can barely keep up with it myself."

"Oh," he said, bending at the waist to wipe a smudge of banana from the corner of Rosie's mouth, "I believe in being thorough, miss."

His hair was steel gray but his eyes were that of a much younger man. She supposed he could have been anywhere between thirty-five and fifty. He stood at least six feet and was the epitome of a British butler.

"Why are you working in a hotel, Andre? Shouldn't you be in London with royalty or something?"

He laid one hand on Rose's head in a loving pat, then looked at Lilah. "I did serve an earl several years ago, but frankly, I grew tired of the cold, gloomy weather in London." He winked again. "It's a lovely place to be *from*, if you understand me."

"Yes," Lilah said with a smile. "I think I do."

"I get back often to visit friends and family and enjoy myself completely on those trips." He folded his hands in front of him and gave a heavy sigh. "Though I must say, I do miss a good pub now and then."

"And I'm going to miss you, Andre," she blurted out, and before she could lose her nerve, came around the table and gave him a hug.

For a second, he went stiff with shock, then relaxed enough to give her a friendly pat on the shoulder. "I shall miss you, as well. Both you and Miss Rose. But this is best for all of you. A child shouldn't grow up in a hotel, after all."

"No, she shouldn't." Lilah looked down at the baby, then thought that Reed shouldn't be locked away in the impersonal suite, either. It couldn't be good for anyone. And that thought brought her back to the day of shopping stretching out in front of her.

She shifted her gaze to the list Andre had given her. "I don't know the stores here at all, so it would be a big help to me if you could tell me which of these is your favorite."

Clearly pleased to be asked his opinion, Andre pointed to the third name on the list. "Lovely leatherwork at that shop. I believe Mr. Hudson would approve."

"Okay, that just got easier. Thank you again," she said as he bowed and turned to leave. She stopped him by saying, "One more question?"

"Of course, miss." He waited patiently.

"I know it's none of my business, but how did a British butler come by the name of Andre?"

A smile flitted across his features quickly, then disappeared. "My mother's father was French. I'm named for him. Caused me quite a bit of trouble as a child, I'm not ashamed to say."

"I'll bet you handled it just fine."

"I like to think so, miss." He bowed again. "Do enjoy your shopping."

When he left, Lilah turned to Rose again. "Oh, yeah, really going to miss him."

A couple of hours later, she was at the furniture shop Andre had recommended and she could silently admit he'd been absolutely right. Reed probably would like what she got here and if he didn't he had no one but himself to blame.

That one brief moment of closeness with Reed at the back of the new house hadn't been repeated and maybe, Lilah told herself, that was just as well. She was caught in a trap—she had to honor her friend's last wish, to have Reed raise the baby, but she wanted Rosie for herself. Basically, she and Reed were standing on opposite sides of a wall and any attempt to breach it—except for dealing with the baby—would be a waste of time.

As if he knew it, too, Reed had been avoiding her as much as possible. It wasn't easy, since they were sharing a hotel suite that, despite its size, seemed to shrink daily. He left for work early every day and didn't get back to the hotel until later in the evening. Usually about the time Lilah was tucking Rose into bed. Accident? Or design? She was willing to bet that Reed deliberately chose to arrive late enough to miss the whole bath time ritual. Then he could claim since the baby was now tucked in and asleep, he wouldn't go in and wake her.

And in spite of all of this? The attraction Lilah felt for him stayed at a slow simmer. The man was clearly uninterested, yet she couldn't seem to convince her body to stop lighting up whenever he walked into a room.

Lilah found it almost impossible to get a read on him.

It was as if he'd accepted his duty in taking Rosie in, but he wasn't going to put any more into it than he absolutely had to.

Not since that first night when he'd scooped Rose out of Lilah's arms to cuddle against his chest had he even once touched her. Held her. Talked to her. Lilah couldn't bear thinking about the kind of life Rosie would have if Reed were simply unable to love her as she needed to be loved. But how could he, when it was clear from everything she'd learned that he and his siblings had grown up without that kind of affection.

Her heart torn, Lilah went through all the motions of what she was supposed to be doing—helping Reed prepare for Rosie being thrust into his life. But furniture and houses and all the money in the world wouldn't make up for a lack of love. She didn't know what she could do, though. She couldn't fight him in court for the baby. Not only was he as rich as Midas, he was a *lawyer*. She wouldn't stand a chance.

So the only hope she had was to somehow break through the wall of ice he'd erected around himself.

"Shouldn't take more than ten or twenty years," she assured herself.

"I'm sorry?"

Lilah flushed, caught talking to herself while her mind wandered. Smiling at the store clerk, she said, "Nothing. Are we about finished here?"

In the past week, with the assistance of the ever-helpful Andre, Lilah and Rose had visited every store she needed to furnish a house she wouldn't be living in. Of course, she had no idea what kind of furniture Reed might prefer, but since he hadn't bothered to give her direction, she'd picked what *she* liked.

Except for one room, a study that would be Reed's territory, Lilah had chosen comfortable furniture, soft colors, all of it coming together to build a warm, safe spot for a little girl to grow up in. Alone, but for a man who wouldn't allow himself to love her.

At that thought, Lilah's heart felt as if it were being squeezed in a cold fist. Soon, she'd be leaving, going back to Utah. She wouldn't be the one taking care of Rosie. Wouldn't be the one to see her walk, hear her first words. She wouldn't be there to dry her tears or hear the baby's giggle first thing in the morning.

She felt the sting of tears in her eyes and quickly blinked to clear them. If she started crying now, the clerk selling her a matching set of twin leather chairs and a sofa for Reed's study would think she was worried about the price. And truly, for the first time in her life, she hadn't even looked at the price tag on any of the furniture.

Normally in this situation, she would have been searching out the best bargain and mentally calculating just how far she could stretch her savings. But with Reed's insistence on blank-check shopping, it was going much faster than it would have ordinarily. Except for a kitchen table and Rosie's room, she was pretty much finished.

"Yes, I'll just print out a receipt for you and delivery instructions for our crew." The man stood and practically danced toward the back room. "I'll only be a minute or two."

"It's fine," she said, glancing down at Rosie, who was two-fisting her bottle.

No wonder the salesman was happy. His commission was no doubt going to be spectacular. With the chairs, sofa, tables, lamps, bookcases and rugs she'd purchased, he could probably take the rest of the month off.

As good as his word, Reed had wangled the keys out of the Realtor just as he said he would. There had been deliveries scheduled every day for the past few days and tomorrow would see the last of them, when this order was taken out to the new house. Beds for the master and three guest bedrooms had already been set up and Rosie's new crib and furnishings would be delivered that afternoon.

By the next day, they would all be living in that house overlooking the ocean. And that, Lilah thought, would just give Reed even *more* room to avoid her and the baby. She had to put a stop to it. Had to ensure that Reed spent time with Rosie. Got to know her. To love her. And if he couldn't?

She didn't have an answer.

Closing her eyes, she winced as instantly a familiar image of Reed flashed into her mind—just as it did whenever she tried to get some sleep. Reed, as he was that first night. Dark hair rumpled, broad, tanned chest naked in the moonlight, drawstring pants dipped low on his hips and bare feet—*why* were bare feet suddenly so sexy? Oh, God. She rubbed the spot between her eyes, hoping to wipe away images she was pretty sure had been permanently etched into her brain.

He was arrogant and bossy, no doubt. Gorgeous and sexy, too. Which only made all of this more difficult than it was already.

It would be so much easier if she could just hate him. But how could she when he had instantly moved to fulfill his late sister's wishes? He had bought a house for Rose. He was changing his life for the baby because it was the right thing to do. Hard to hate a man who could do all that.

But if he didn't open his heart to Rose, did anything else matter? God, it felt as if her mind were on an automatic loop, going over and over the same things, day after day with no solution. The man was taking up way too many of her thoughts and that just had to stop.

Lilah gave a quick glance at the clock on the wall. She had to get moving. There were still things like pots, pans, dishes, glassware, throw pillows, comforters and a million other, smaller things to arrange for.

And oh, how she wished her friend Kate was in town to help with all of this. Kate Duffy was an artist, with the kind of eye for decorating that Lilah lacked. Kate would have mowed through every art gallery, department store and lighting shop and, in a blink, would have seen exactly what should go where in the beautiful house on the cliff. But, Kate was on her long-delayed honeymoon with a military husband finally back from deployment.

So, she was in this alone.

A clatter of sound interrupted her thoughts and Lilah looked at Rose in her stroller, happily slamming her bottle against the tray in front of her. The tiny girl grinned and babbled wildly.

Laughing, Lilah leaned over, kissed the baby's cheek and whispered, "You're absolutely right. I'm not alone at all, am I?"

"All right then, Ms. Strong..." The salesman was back, full of bright cheer that spoke of the giant commission he was about to make. "Paperwork is right here. If you'll sign at the bottom..."

She quickly read over the receipt, then signed her name. "Everything will be delivered tomorrow?"

"Between one and three."

"Okay, thank you."

"Oh, my pleasure." He dipped into the breast pocket of his jacket, pulled out a card and handed it to her. "If you need anything else…"

"Thanks again." She took the card, dropped it into her purse, then left, pushing Rosie's stroller out onto the sidewalk.

June in Southern California could be either gloomy or beautiful, and today was definitely one of the pretty ones. The sidewalks were crowded, and the narrow streets were packed with impatient drivers tapping horns as if doing it could clear traffic. Flower-filled baskets hung from old-fashioned streetlights and teenagers with surfboards tucked beneath their arms bolted across the street toward the ocean.

It was all so far from the familiar, Lilah felt a pang of homesickness that was wiped away by the sound of Rosie's crow of delight. What was she going to do in her quiet house when there was no Rose to shatter the silence? How would she handle being so far away from the baby who felt like her own?

"Problems to face later," Lilah said, deliberately shoving those troubling thoughts aside to get on with her day. There were still so many things to do and she was running out of time.

While Lilah shopped like a woman on a mission, Reed pushed through his own commitments. He filed divorce papers with the court, settled his bill with the hotel and arranged for people to pack and move his stuff to the new house. And now, he had to spend some time reassuring Carson Duke.

"Have you talked to Tia?" Reed asked, following the other man with his gaze as he paced the confines of his suite at the Monarch.

For the first time, Reed noticed that one suite was pretty much like the other. Yes, his own was much bigger than this one, but the furnishings were very similar. And Carson looked ill at ease as he moved through the slash of sunlight pouring through the glass terrace doors.

"No," Carson muttered, shoving one hand through his hair. "Haven't talked to her since I moved out of our place a month ago."

"Keep it that way," Reed advised. He'd dealt with divorcing couples for enough years to know that even a split that started out amicable could turn into a battle. And then the case would be judged in the media, fueled by stealthy camera shots taken by the ever-hungry paparazzi.

Carson stopped, shoved both hands into his jeans and nodded. "I know that's the right strategy. But I can't help feeling that if we could talk—"

"Did talking help either of you the last few months?" His voice was deliberately impatient. If he offered sympathy here, his client wouldn't be able to do what was best for him. Better to be firm with his advice.

He frowned. "No. No, it didn't."

Reed took a sip of coffee, then set his cup down on the low glass table in front of him. "I know this is hard, but it's what you've both decided to do. You're better off not speaking with Tia until the court proceedings are done. With your prenup in place, this should be a painless situation to resolve."

"Painless."

Reed nodded. He prided himself on getting his clients through the end of a marriage with as little pain as possible. "Not completely, but this should move along with few complications."

"That's good, I guess," Carson said with a wry smile. "Didn't imagine I'd be in this position, I've got to say."

"No one does," Reed assured him.

Carson snorted. "Maybe. I do know that not growing up in Hollywood made me believe that people can choose to stay together. To work at it. Hell, my own parents have been married forever. They're still happy."

And Reed couldn't help wondering what that was like. Naturally, in his business, he didn't run into long-term marriages. He had no personal experience with it, either. How had it felt to grow up, as Carson had, with one set of parents? Hell, Reed had so many official and honorary grandparents, he couldn't keep track of them all.

The extended Hudson family hadn't exactly been the "norm" or even close to ideal. But it was what he knew.

"So, when can I expect to be a free man again?"

Reed looked at Carson. "Well, you've been married less than two years, and have no children, so that makes things less complicated."

"Happy to help," the man muttered.

Reed understood what Carson was feeling, so he simply went on, "You do own property together…"

"Yeah," Carson said. "The Malibu beach house and a cabin in Montana."

Nodding, Reed said, "Once Tia signs the papers as well, I'll meet with her attorney and we go into what's called *discovery*. That's laying out all jointly held properties and bank accounts and so forth…"

Carson swiped one hand across his face, but nodded solemnly. "And then?"

Smiling, Reed said, "*Then* we prepare a marital settlement agreement and if you both agree with the terms, you'll sign and six months after that, you'll be single again."

"Will we have to go to court?"

"Depends on how the settlement agreement goes. We could end up in a mediator's office, or be seen by a judge."

"Right." Carson coughed out a laugh and shook his head. "I swear, I just never thought Tia and I would end up this way." He shot Reed a look. "You probably hear that all the time."

"Not really," Reed said. "People don't come to divorce lawyers wanting to talk about how good their relationship is."

"Guess not." Carson turned to look out at the ocean. "I thought we'd be different. Thought we'd make it. Hell, Tia even loves my parents." He shook his head again. "Don't know how we ended up here."

"You may never know," Reed said, and stood up. "And trying to dissect the whole thing won't give you peace."

Carson turned his head and looked at him. "What will?"

Reed gave him a grim smile. "If I find out, I'll let you know."

"Right. Okay. Look, I appreciate your bringing me the papers…"

"No problem. I live here, remember?"

"Yeah, but I don't, so I'll be leaving this afternoon." He blew out a breath. "I've got to get back to Hollywood.

Have an early call Monday and there are a few things I have to do over the weekend."

"New movie?" Reed asked.

"No, just a few reshoots on the last one," Carson said. "Back to make-believe and pretense. Today I'm just a guy, Monday morning I'm a Viking again. Weird way to make a living."

"There are weirder." Reed didn't remind the other man that essentially, at its core, he made a living dissolving people's lives. In Reed's book, that made for much stranger than pretending to be a Viking. With that dark thought circling his brain, he buttoned his suit coat and said, "If you need anything, you know where to reach me. Otherwise, I'll be in touch."

"Right."

"And steer clear of Tia," Reed said again, knowing the warning was necessary.

"Yeah, I will." Carson flashed the grin he was famous for. "If I'd done that a couple years ago, I wouldn't be in this mess, right?"

"True." Harsh, Reed knew, and he saw that single word slam home with Carson. But the simple reality was that divorce was the main reason to avoid marriage in the first place.

If that point hadn't been hammered into him watching his own family's near legendary divorce battles, then it would have been over the past several years. Leading his clients through sometimes messy and always miserable dissolutions. Hell, watching Carson Duke right now was just one more reinforcement of the decision Reed had made long ago to remain single.

"Thanks," Carson said. "For everything."

"Just doing my job," Reed told him, then headed out to take care of the mess his own life had recently become. But with any luck, he was about to smooth some of those choppy waters.

An hour later, he was at the new house and had to admit that Lilah had done a good job of furnishing the place. It looked…settled, he supposed, as if everything had been in place for years, not days. *Years.* Damn, that sounded…*permanent.* If he concentrated, Reed would probably be able to actually *feel* roots sprouting up through the floor of the house to wrap around his ankles like chains. Which was exactly why Reed had never bought a house before this. He hadn't wanted to be tied to anything. Along with avoiding marriage, he'd avoided commitments to *places*, as well.

He'd always kept his options open, so that even if he'd never packed up and left town at a moment's notice, he'd always known that he *could.* But now, that was over. He was a homeowner. Or would be by tomorrow. He would have roots for the first time in his life, and that thought felt almost like a noose slowly tightening around his neck.

Hardly surprising, since between boarding schools and vacation homes and the change of address every time his parents remarried, Reed had never had a childhood "home." At least not one where memories were made. He didn't have a particular love of any one place due to a connection to the past. He lived in a hotel so he could leave whenever he wanted to. And now…well, that was over.

The house itself, though, was fine. Glancing around

the great room, Reed approved. Lilah'd promised color and she hadn't lied, but he had to admit that the overall effect was, he supposed, homey. There were heavy rugs in deep jewel tones and oversize furniture covered in soft colors of cream and pale blue. There were lamps and tables and even some of his own art from the hotel hanging on the walls. Odd, he hadn't even noticed them missing from the suite, yet somehow Lilah had managed to have them boxed, moved and hung.

He heard the rumbles of conversation floating to him from different areas of the house. Movers were there, setting up the nursery, and the surprise he'd arranged for was no doubt getting acquainted with Lilah.

He had to give her full points. She'd done a lot of work in very little time. She would absolutely have been worth the money he'd offered to pay her. He still couldn't believe that she'd refused a hundred thousand dollars. Especially when he knew she could use it.

Reed had done some research on his own. He'd looked into her business—you could find anything if you knew where to look. Lilah's Bouquet was a small company with a few employees and a well-laid-out website for online business. Who knew there were so many buyers for pretty soaps and candles? She owned a home with a reasonable mortgage, a ten-year-old car and was, as far as he could tell, well liked and respected in her incredibly small hometown. No family but her parents, and a year or two after her father's death, her mother had remarried a millionaire, so maybe that was the reason behind Lilah's turning down money from him.

Whatever lay behind it, though, he knew she was staying not because he'd asked it of her, but because she was looking out for Rose. Hard to blame her for that. In fact, he appreciated it. He just didn't like being in anyone's debt.

And until he had this new situation locked down and sewed up, he would owe Lilah Strong.

# Five

She came into the room just then as if thinking of her had conjured her. A wide smile was on her expressive face, and her eyes were shining. That amazing hair of hers tumbled in waves and curls and bounced with her every step.

"Okay, she's wonderful," Lilah said.

Satisfaction welled inside him. The surprise he'd arranged had gone off better than he'd thought it would. If he had to say it himself, he'd had a stroke of genius in coaxing his mother's former housekeeper-slash-nanny out of semiretirement.

Connie Thomas was in her early sixties, loved kids and had the organizational skills of a four-star general. For more than twenty-five years, Connie had been the one constant in Reed's life. She'd stayed with them through his mother's many marriages and even more frequent moves. Connie was the one the kids in the family went to when they were in trouble or lonely or just needed a sympathetic ear. She'd finally decided to leave, though, when Reed's mother decided her youngest son, at seven, didn't really need to come home from boarding school for the summer.

His mother wasn't the most maternal woman in the known world, and even as he thought it, Reed felt a pang of guilt. She loved her kids, he knew, but in an abstracted way that didn't necessarily require her children's presence. In fact, Selena Taylor-Hudson-Simmons-Foster-Hambleton had never understood how Connie Thomas had so much patience for kids.

"Rosie is already crazy about her," Lilah was saying. "So of course I am."

He nodded. "I suspected you'd approve."

"How could I not?" Lilah was smiling up at him, and it bothered Reed just how much he liked it. "Connie and the baby hit it off instantly." Taking a deep breath, she went on, "And you should know that Connie loves her suite of rooms off the kitchen. She told me you've arranged to have her things delivered here tonight."

"No point in waiting, is there?"

A short chuckle shot from her. "Not for you—and apparently not for Connie, either. Right now, she's taken Rosie upstairs to 'supervise' the movers setting things up in the nursery."

He wasn't surprised to hear that. Connie wasn't one to sit back and let things happen around her. She liked to have her hand in things.

"She'll drive the movers crazy, but she'll be satisfied with their work before she lets them leave."

"You make her sound like a drill sergeant," Lilah said, tipping her head to one side to look up at him.

"She could be," he admitted, then smiled, remembering. "She was the one who made sure baths were taken, homework was done and teeth were brushed. She also kept the cookie jar filled with her magic chocolate chip bars."

"Magic?" Lilah asked quietly.

"Seemed like magic at the time," he said. "Never had anything taste as good as those cookie bars did." Funny, a few minutes ago, he'd been thinking that he really had no memories of a *home*. But now, his mind filled with images of Connie, making cookies, playing board games with the younger kids in the family. Showing them how to make their own beds and expecting them to do it by reminding them all that the maids worked for their parents, *not* for them.

All the kids in the house had known they would find sympathy, understanding and honesty in Connie's kitchen. Reed had benefited more than once from the woman's no-nonsense view of the world. He couldn't imagine his childhood without her. Smiling, he said, "Yeah, those bars were magic."

"Can't wait to try them." Lilah tipped her head to one side and watched him. "There's more than cookies to your memories, though, isn't there?"

Frowning, he realized she was reading him and he didn't like it. "She's a good person. That's all."

"Uh-huh."

"Look," he said, trying to counter the patient expression on her face, "I'm not looking to learn and share and grow here. There is nothing to this beyond Connie being the most logical solution to our current problem."

"There it is again," Lilah said softly. "Rose isn't a problem to solve."

He stiffened a bit under the criticism. "Her care is."

"So now that Connie's here, you're off the hook in the care department?" Lilah cocked her head and stared up at him through eyes that seemed to have a laser focus. "Is that how it works?"

How the hell had he gone from a hero—bringing Connie here—to the bad guy, for the same damn reason? Beginning to be seriously irritated now, Reed countered, "If you've got something to say, say it."

She shook her head. "Where to begin?"

"Just start," he said, voice clipped. Folding his arms across his chest, he stood in the center of his brand-new living room and waited.

"Fine." She took a deep breath, looked him square in the eye and said, "In the week Rosie and I have been here, you've hardly spent any time at all with her."

He snorted. "In case you haven't noticed, I do have work."

"Oh, hard not to notice," Lilah said. "You're always gone. And on the rare moments you are around, you keep a very real distance between you and Rosie."

Truth hit home, but he didn't feel the need to defend himself against it, either. "There is no distance, for God's sake. I'm her uncle. She's my sister's daughter. I just bought her a *house*. I think it's safe to say that I'm inserting her into my life."

"Why does she have to be inserted?" Lilah asked.

"Because she's never been here before?" Reed countered, his voice lowering to a growl.

"That's not what I meant. You can't just shove her into your old life. You and she need to build a *new* life together." Waving her hands a little as if to encompass the living room, she said, "Buying a house is great. But if that's all it is, it's not enough."

Irritation spiked into a sizzle of resentment that caught and burned at the base of his throat. Since this woman and the baby had walked into his life a week ago, everything he knew had been turned inside out. But apparently, that wasn't enough for Lilah Strong.

Reed gave her the cold-eyed glare he usually reserved for hostile witnesses or clients who tried to lie to him. "She's eight months old. What more does she need? A car? A boat?"

"A *home*."

"What the hell is that supposed to mean?" The tight rein on his temper was strained. He knew that Connie, the baby and the last of the deliverymen were just upstairs. Damned if he'd have an argument the whole world could listen in on.

"It means, buying a *house* doesn't make it a *home*."

"Unbelievable." He shook his head. "You're wasting your time making fancy soaps. You should be writing poems for a greeting card company."

"This isn't funny." Her voice was as cool and flat as his own.

"You got that right." He expected her to back down, to smooth over and try for cool reason. He was wrong.

She moved in on him and he could see actual *sparks* flashing in her eyes. "*Your* life isn't the only one that has been 'disrupted.' Rosie has lost her mother. I have lost my friend. I'm a few hundred miles from home and doing my best to keep Rosie safe and happy."

"I get that," he interrupted.

"Not finished," she continued, taking another step closer. "You've avoided me and Rosie all week."

His back teeth ground together. Yeah, he had, but he hadn't expected her to notice. After all, he was a busy man and God knew she'd had plenty to do. "Not avoiding—"

"Ignoring then," she said quickly. "Comes to the same thing. The point is, a house won't be enough. Connie, as great as she is, won't be enough."

Sunlight slanted over her hair, picking up the gold in the red and making it shine. Today she smelled like orange blossoms, and that scent was clogging his throat and fogging his mind. That was the only explanation for him standing there taking a lecture as he hadn't had since he was eighteen and had displeased his father.

"She needs love. Affection. A sense of belonging."

Shaking his head, he felt the first tiny thread of worry begin to snake along his spine. "She'll have everything she needs."

"How can she when you haven't so much as looked at her since that first night?"

"I don't need you to teach me how to take care of a child." And even if he did need the help, damned if he'd ask for it.

She took a deep breath and tried to calm herself. He could almost hear her thinking, *Yelling at him is no way to get through to him.* She'd be right about that.

"All I'm trying to say is," she said, voice patient enough to spike his irritation meter, "I'm staying until I know Rosie is safe and loved and happy. That's not going to happen until you start interacting with her."

"She's a baby," he said tightly. "She's happy if she's fed and dry."

"She needs more than that—she needs family, a sense of belonging. I don't see that coming from you."

Reed wasn't used to being questioned. Doubted. His clients all believed in him. His family turned to him for every crisis imaginable, trusting him to take care of things. Hell, he'd lived his life accepting responsibility and doing everything he could to make sure the world rolled on in an organized way.

Did she really believe an eight-month-old baby would defeat him? His tone was patient and he gave himself points for that, since inside, he was seething. "Rose will get everything she needs."

"From Connie?" she asked.

"Yeah, from Connie. I brought in the one woman I *know* will do right by her. How is that a bad thing?" He took a deep breath and instantly regretted it since that orange scent clinging to her seemed to be invading him.

"It's bad if you depend solely on her to care for Rose."

"I didn't say I would."

"Actions speak louder than words," she pointed out. "And what you're doing is ignoring me and Rose."

"I'm not ignoring the baby. I'm ignoring *you*."

"Why?" she demanded, tossing both hands high.

Could she really not see what it cost him to avoid her company? Was she clueless about the attraction sizzling between them? Well, if so, Reed thought, it was time to let her know exactly what was going on here.

Her scent reached for him, surrounded him and he threw caution out the damn window. "Because of this."

He grabbed her, pulled her in close and kissed her as he'd wanted to for days.

Lilah hadn't expected *this*.

He'd moved so fast, pulled her in so close, held her so tight.

And, oh, my God, his *mouth.*

Reed kissed her with a hunger she'd never experienced before. And for one split second, she was too stunned, too shocked, to do anything more than stand there. But when that second passed, she was kissing him back.

Her body jumped into life, as if she'd somehow been electrocuted. There was a hot jolt of...*everything* blasting through her. Lilah's arms linked around his neck, she leaned into him and parted her lips beneath his. The sweep of his tongue took her breath and sent even more jagged slices of lightning through her body.

A hot ball of need settled in the pit of her stomach and even lower a throbbing ache awoke, and breathless, she knew she wanted, needed, *more.*

His big hands swept up and down her back, pulling her closer, until she felt as if she wanted to simply melt into his body. He cupped her behind and held her tightly to him until she felt the hardness of his body pressing into hers. The need jangling within jumped into high gear, sending her heartbeat into a thundering gallop. Tingling head to toe, Lilah could have stayed exactly where she was for, oh...eternity.

But even as she thought it, other sounds intruded through the buzzing in her ears. Voices, getting louder. Footsteps, coming closer.

And in a rush, her brain suddenly shrieked a warning, reminding her that the house was filled with moving men, not to mention Connie and Rose.

It took every ounce of control she had for Lilah to break away and take a long step back from temptation. Struggling to catch her breath, she knew what she must look like—eyes wide, hair tangled from his busy fingers running through it, mouth swollen from a kiss like no other. There was nothing she could do about that, though, so she instead fought to slow her heart rate and get her body back under control. Not easy since it felt as if every single cell in her body was wide awake and sending up skyrockets in anticipation.

It had been way too long since she'd been with a man. That had to be the reason she'd…overreacted like that. Running her own business didn't give her much time to look for and develop a love life. At least that was the excuse she usually gave herself. But the truth was, she simply hadn't found a man she was interested in enough to make a try at a relationship.

Not that Reed was the one for her. She already knew that was going nowhere, although, after that kiss, she had to admit that maybe he felt something for her whether he wanted to or not. But even if he did, he was rich and lived in California, while she lived in a tiny mountain town and was substantially less than wealthy. They were from completely different worlds and one kiss—no matter how amazing—wasn't enough to bridge the gap. Best to remember that.

"All finished," a deep voice announced as three moving men walked into the main room.

"Just in time," Lilah muttered. She glanced briefly at Reed, saw the flash of banked lust in his eyes then told herself not to look at him again. At least not until the fire inside her had died down. Shouldn't take more than a week or two.

Oh, God.

Things had just gotten so much more complicated. Maybe it would have been better for him to go right on ignoring her. But it was probably too late to go back now.

They were going to have to talk about this, Lilah told herself. Come to an agreement that there would be no more kissing, and wasn't that a sad thought? But Rose had to be the priority. For both of them.

"Right, I'll just go and check everything," she said, taking the excuse the movers had handed her and running with it.

Connie was just walking into the room, a happy, babbling Rosie on her hip. The baby held out her arms to Lilah and in response, she scooped her up and kept walking. The warm, solid weight of the baby in her arms was the perfect antidote to the still-pulsing need she felt inside. Rose was the reason she was here. The *only* reason. Her happiness was paramount.

In the newly setup nursery, Lilah did a quick inspection, made sure the furniture had all been put together and set where she'd told Connie she wanted them. If she took a couple of extra minutes to cool down, who was to know? Finally, though, she headed back to the main room.

There, she found two of the movers had already gone out to their truck. Since Reed had no idea what furniture she'd purchased, Lilah was the one who signed the delivery and setup sheet the remaining mover held out to her. When she was finished, she closed the door behind him and took a slow, steadying breath before heading into the great room to join Reed and Connie.

"Everything all right in here?" the woman asked, her gaze darting from Reed to Lilah and back again.

"Yeah, fine," Reed said, scraping one hand along his jaw.

"Dandy," Lilah agreed, keeping her gaze locked on the baby in her arms.

"Uh-huh," Connie said with a shake of her head. "You two are terrible liars."

She walked over, plucked Rosie from Lilah's grasp and headed for the kitchen. "I'm just going to give this sweet baby a snack. While we're busy, the two of you can talk about whatever it is that's not happening."

Alone with him in the great room, Lilah listened to the silence for a couple of long minutes before finally giving a sigh and muttering, "That's just great."

"What's the problem?"

She looked at Reed. "Really? You kiss me brainless and then your housekeeper takes one look at me and knows what's been going on and you wonder what the problem is?"

He shrugged. "It was just a kiss."

"Yeah. And Godiva is just chocolate." She pushed both hands through her hair then faced him. She didn't mean to stare at his mouth, it just…happened. God. They really did need to talk. And it looked as though it was going to have to be her opening the conversation.

She lifted her gaze to his and asked, "Why?"

He waved the question off. "Why not?"

Well, didn't she feel special? Then something occurred to her and Lilah inhaled sharply, narrowed her eyes on him. "Did you kiss me just to shut me up?"

Now his green eyes flashed and a muscle in his jaw ticked. "What?"

"We were arguing," she reminded him and warmed to her idea as she kept talking. "You were losing, so you wanted me quiet."

Reed laughed shortly and shook his head. "Again, I'll remind you I'm an attorney. I argue for a living. I wasn't losing."

"Oh, please," she said, giving him a satisfied smile. Connie was right. Reed really was a terrible liar. Which meant she was, too, but that wasn't the point right now. "We both know I was right. You've been ignoring Rosie, avoiding me. I called you on it and you didn't like it. So to end the argument, you kissed me."

He took a step closer and Lilah just managed to not take an equal step back. She wasn't afraid of him or anything. She just didn't know if being too close to him right that moment was the best possible idea. Yet backing up would make him think she didn't trust herself around him. Which she didn't—but why let him know that?

"I don't have to kiss a woman to win an argument. I make a lot of money by winning arguments." His gaze moved over her features before meeting her eyes again. "You want the truth? I kissed you because I wanted to. And like I told you once before, when I want something, I go get it."

Well, that was both insulting and flattering. For a week now, she'd been fighting her attraction to Reed, knowing it couldn't go anywhere. Knowing it would just complicate an already out-of-control situation. And boy had she been right.

In her own imagination, a kiss between them would have been hot, leaving them both uncomfortable. In reality, the kiss was well beyond hot and had left them both...wary. Plus, now she couldn't help wondering what sex with him would be like. But as soon as that thought jumped merrily into her mind, she pushed it back out again. As hard as it would be, she was going to forget all about this kiss and the way he'd made her feel for a few shining moments. It was the only way to survive being around him.

"I'm not a prize you can grab off a shelf, Reed. And if I don't want you to kiss me again, you won't, believe me."

"Not much of a threat." His voice was a dark rumble that seemed to settle along her spine and vibrate. "Since you already want me to kiss you again."

Lilah took a deep breath and let it slide from her lungs on a long sigh. She could lie, but what would be the point? He'd felt her reaction to his kiss. He could probably look into her eyes right now and still see the smoldering embers of the inferno he'd started inside her.

"Fine. Okay, maybe I do want you to kiss me." He moved in on her and this time she *did* skip backward out of reach. If she let him touch her right now, he'd set off a chain reaction within her that would quickly flare up out of control. If she was going to draw a line in the sand, then it had to be here and now. "But unlike you, I don't go after something just because I want it."

A barely there smile touched one corner of his mouth. "Is that right?"

She squared her shoulders, lifted her chin and told herself she was doing the right thing. "Absolutely. We don't always want what's good for us."

He laughed shortly, tucked his hands into his pockets and nodded. "Truer words," he mused.

Lilah's eyebrows arched. She was pretty sure she'd just been insulted. "Thanks very much."

As if he could read the tension spiraling through her, he took a step back, then another. "Look, I've told you my father doesn't want the baby and Spring's mother says she simply can't do it because she would miss Spring too much, though she also pointed out she's not interested in being a grandma. So I'm keeping Rose. Raising her."

"Loving her?" Lilah had to ask. Had to make him see that money and a roof over her head would not be enough to give Rose the whole, complete life she deserved.

He frowned at her. "What is this obsession you have with love?"

"Obsession?" she repeated. "What is your fierce opposition to it?"

"I've seen too many people crushed because love was taken away. Or denied. Or tossed aside. Love," he said, voice dark, deep, "is the root of every misery in the world."

"That's a sad attitude."

"And I earned it," he told her, shaking his head, walking across the room to look out the window at the neatly tended front yard.

He didn't speak again, but Lilah was intrigued enough by his silence to follow him. To try to find the first chink in the wall he surrounded himself with. "How? How did you earn the right to say that love is worthless?"

Glancing at her, he said, "I've had a front-row seat my whole damn life to the show of my parents constantly looking for and never finding this mysterious 'love.' They discard wives and husbands like most people change cars and never once have they found what they're looking for.

"My brothers, sisters and I were caught up in the resulting chaos." He turned to face her. "So no, I can't promise love. And I'd like to say that I really don't require your approval for how I raise my niece."

"I know," she said, though those two simple words left a bitter taste in her mouth. "But this isn't about only you, Reed. This is about what's best for Rosie."

"I know that, which is why you're still here." He loosened his tie, then shrugged out of his suit jacket and tossed it behind him to the arm of the sofa. When he looked at her again, he said, "You've got some idea of what my life with Rose should be. News flash—no kid has a perfect life. I've got a demanding job with long hours. Doesn't leave a lot of time for building a nest, for God's sake."

"You don't have to—I already have," she said, sweeping one hand out to encompass the living room and the rest of the house besides. "But you will have to make some changes for Rose's sake."

He laughed shortly. "I'd say we're both standing in the middle of a pretty damn big change."

"Yes, but—"

"And Connie's here now." He glanced past her toward the hall that led to the kitchen. "Trust me when I say Rose couldn't have a better person taking care of her."

"I believe that," Lilah said, since spending just a few minutes with Connie had convinced her that the woman was a born nurturer. "Okay, yes, Rosie will get plenty of care and affection from Connie. But you're her father figure."

He scowled at her.

She saw the flicker of what might have been panic in his eyes and actually felt better seeing it. "You are the man in her life and you have to *be* in her life—not just some ghost who drifts in and out."

She watched a muscle in his jaw twitch and flex and she knew how hard this was for him. There probably weren't many people in Reed Hudson's life who were willing to stand toe-to-toe with him over anything. And maybe she wouldn't have been either, ordinarily. But this was about Rose's future, so she was willing to do what she had to. Didn't seem to matter that her mouth was still buzzing from that kiss or that her nerves were still tangled together in slippery knots.

"You know," he said, "I don't much like taking orders."

"I didn't mean—"

"Oh, yeah, you did," he said and loomed over her, maybe hoping to intimidate her. But Lilah just met him glare for glare.

Seconds ticked past and the silence stretched out between them.

"Why do you smell different every day?" he murmured, and the irritation in his eyes shifted to something hotter, more intimate.

"What?" The abrupt shift in conversation had her shaking her head, trying to catch up.

"Your scent," he repeated, moving in and drawing a deep breath. "It's oranges today." He laid both hands on her shoulders and then skimmed his hands up along her neck to cup her face in his palms.

God, she felt the heat of him sliding down into her system, again, and she shivered with the rush of it. This was not a good idea. Hadn't she *just* told him that he wouldn't be kissing her again. Ever? And here she was, sliding into that puddle of want just because he touched her.

"It's driving me crazy," he admitted, his voice no more than a whisper now. His gaze locked on hers. "Every day, there's a new scent clinging to you and I wake up wondering what it's going to be. Then I have to get close enough to you to taste it. And," he added, as he dipped his head to hers, "once I'm close I don't want to be anywhere else."

"It's my soaps," she whispered, amazed that she could talk with his mouth no more than a breath from hers. With the golden sunlight streaming through the window, wrapping them both in a slash of light that seemed to glow with warmth.

"Yeah," he said, "I figured that out. And now I know that when you're rubbing that scent all over you, you're wet and naked."

She took a long, slow breath and her stomach did a quick spin. He was going to pull her in again, she knew it. He knew it. Maybe she'd stand a chance against him and what he made her feel if she turned and sprinted from the room. But she wasn't entirely sure her legs would support her. So she had to try for reason instead.

"Okay, maybe we should just stop…"

"Yeah," he agreed. "Maybe we should. But we're not going to."

"No, I don't think we are."

# Six

A tiny voice in the back of Lilah's mind shouted that it would be much better for this situation if they could keep their distance. But she'd never felt anything like this incredible heat, this indescribable need, so she silently told that logical little voice to be quiet and go away.

This was ridiculous. She knew it. But she couldn't help the wanting. Her heart hammered in her chest. Breath caught in her lungs and her body felt as if she were on fire. This man had way too much power over her. One touch from him was a storm of sensation and the need for more clamored inside her.

"This isn't solving anything," she managed to say.

"Yeah, I know." He took her mouth again and instantly Lilah's thoughts dissolved into a murky puddle.

She met him eagerly, wrapping her around him, holding on as her body trembled and quaked from too many sensations pouring in at once. His hands dropped from her face to explore her curves with a rough sense of urgency that felt like gasoline being poured on a fire. Up and down her spine, down to her bottom and back up to cup her breasts, his hands seemed to be everywhere at once. She groaned and even that small sound was muffled by the roaring in her ears.

The house was quiet, only adding to the feeling of intimacy. And though it felt as if they were alone in the house, they really weren't, and a moment later, both of them remembered it.

The baby's wail shattered their kiss and broke them apart in an instant.

"What the hell?" Reed demanded, clearly horrified. "It sounds like she's being tortured."

"No." Lilah choked out a laugh and pushed her hair back from her face with shaking hands. "She's just past her nap time."

"Good God."

The appalled look on his face brought another short laugh from her. He was clearly clueless about babies and now was as good a time as any to start his education. Still a little unsteady on her feet, Lilah reached out and patted his chest. "I'll be right back."

She left him, headed for the kitchen. A few deep breaths helped her steady herself, though she figured her stomach would be jumping and her heart racing for quite a while yet. Once inside, she found Connie patting Rose's back and murmuring to her. Glancing up at Lilah, she said, "She's tired, poor thing."

"It's way past her nap time," Lilah agreed. "If we had food and any of her things already here, we could just put her down upstairs. But we'll get her back to the hotel."

"Good idea," Connie said, handing the baby over. "While you three are gone, I'll get groceries and things and have everything ready for all of you to settle in tomorrow."

Rose dropped her head on Lilah's shoulder, but the crying didn't stop. Sliding her hand up and down Rose's back, Lilah gave Connie a grateful smile. "I'm really glad you're going to be a part of Rose's life, Connie."

"Me, too," the older woman said, already beginning to bustle around the model-home-perfect kitchen, making it her own. "Retirement's for old people. I was bored stiff to tell the truth." Humming to herself, she set about rearranging the cupboards and didn't even notice when Lilah and Rosie left the room.

"It's okay, sweetie," Lilah crooned, giving the baby a soft jiggle as she walked down the hall back toward the main room where she'd left Reed.

The comforting, warm weight of Rose's small body pressed to hers made Lilah's heart sigh with love—even while she tried to imagine living without it. That thought was dark enough to make her eyes sting, but she blinked back tears that wouldn't do her any good. The house was cozy, in spite of its size, and she knew that Rose would love living here. Lilah only wished that she could be there, to watch Rose grow, to be a part of her life.

Walking into the great room, she watched Reed turn at the sound of Rose's sniffling cry. His eyes were shining, but wary.

*Perfect*, Lilah thought. She knew he wasn't immune to Rose. She'd seen him that first night, after all, when he'd cuddled her close. And she could understand the caution she sensed in him. But until he let himself truly care for Rose, that wariness would always be with him.

It was part of the wall he'd built around himself. He'd already told her about what growing up with a very different family had been like for him. So she couldn't really blame him for being suspicious of love. But wasn't it long overdue for him to put his past behind him?

"Is she all right?" he asked.

"She's fine," Lilah said, still stroking the crying baby's back. "Just tired."

"Then we should go." He grabbed his suit jacket off the sofa and shrugged into it. "Give me the keys to your rental. I'll bring it around to the front and you can strap her in for the drive back to the hotel."

"Yeah." She walked up to him and plopped Rose into his arms, giving him no choice but to hold the tiny girl. "I'll bring the car around, then you can strap her in."

He looked like a man caught in a trap. Shifting the baby to his shoulder, he looked at her. "I don't—"

"Look," Lilah interrupted. "She's even stopped crying for you." *Good girl, Rosie*, she thought. "Won't take me a minute to get the car."

She hurriedly left the room, but paused at the threshold long enough to glance back. Reed and Rose stood in a slash of sunlight, each of them staring at the other as if discovering a new world. And maybe, she thought as she left the house, that's exactly what they were doing.

They settled into the house with hardly a bump.

Reed spent every day buried in paperwork, handholding clients and thinking about the woman currently living in his house. For the first time in his memory, his concentration was shattered. Reed went through the motions, going to court, meeting with mediators and advising his clients, yet there was one corner of his mind not focused on the job at all. Instead, it was centered on Lilah Strong and what she was doing to him.

Memories of kisses that never should have happened continued to bubble and burn at the back of his mind, tormenting him during the day and torturing him at night. He couldn't sleep, and even work didn't have the same draw for him as it had before.

His life had been thrown into turmoil and there was only one way to get everything back into order. Lilah wouldn't leave until she knew that Rosie would be happy. So, the way to make her go the hell home and let him get back to his normal life was to prove to her that he and Rose would get along without her.

And fine, he could admit she'd had a point about getting to know Rose. He couldn't stand back from a child he'd agreed to raise. Even not counting the problem of Lilah, Reed had to get comfortable with the baby who was now a part of his life.

Which was why he was bent over a bathtub, getting just as wet as the infant sitting in a few inches of warm, bubble-filled water.

"She doesn't think we can do this." Reed kept one cautious hand lightly against Rose's back as she splashed gleefully in the tub. Her tiny feet kicked up a storm, making frantic waves while she laughed and turned her shining eyes up to him.

Unexpectedly, Reed's heart gave a hard *thump* in his chest as he looked down into her bright green gaze. Until tonight, she'd been more or less a shadow to him. He knew she was there of course, but their interactions had been limited—purposely. He'd deliberately avoided contact with her because he hadn't wanted to *care*. Caring was an open doorway to misery, pain, fear and all kinds of dark possibilities.

And as his heart continued to squeeze in his chest, he realized that he was in it now. A few minutes alone with a child who looked up at him as if he was her personal hero was enough to start him down the road he'd managed to sidestep most of his life.

She was so small, yet already, Rose was her own little person with a grin that caught at your heart and a temper that could set off a screech strong enough to peel paint off walls. Weirdly, Reed liked knowing she had that strong personality. She wouldn't be a pushover, that was for sure. She'd stand up for herself.

But he'd be there, too. His course was set and whether Lilah believed it or not, Reed knew his life was never again going to be what it had been. "I'll make sure you're safe, Rose."

The baby giggled, and that deep, rolling, straight-up-from-the-gut sound settled into his chest and gave his heart another hard squeeze.

"You're going to tear me up, aren't you?" He smoothed the soft washcloth over her back, and then around to her narrow chest while she slapped the water, sending droplets flying to splatter his shirt and face.

"Yeah, you are. You're a heartbreaker. It's in your eyes and you're already working on me." He sighed a little as the baby laughed and then gently ran the flat of his hand over her damp curly hair.

It had been inevitable, he told himself. From the moment Lilah had carried Spring's daughter into his office, he'd been headed exactly *here*. Somewhere deep inside, he'd known that Rose would be able to breach his defenses. He'd spent most of his life with the determination to keep from caring too much about anyone. He loved his brothers and sisters of course, but even there he maintained a distance. Just enough to protect himself. But this one baby with her happy smile and trusting eyes could undo him. Reed blew out a breath and tried to accept his new reality. But if he was still fighting it just a little, who could blame him?

"Time to get out," he said with a sudden laugh as Rose kicked and slapped all at once and splashed water into her own face. Her tiny features screwed up, the smile disappeared and she blinked frantically. "Not as much fun when you're the one getting splashed, is it?"

She looked up at him, her mouth turned down, and he knew he was about to be deafened by a screech. Quickly, he snatched her up out of the water and, using only one hand, wrapped a towel around her as he cuddled her to his chest. "Hey, you're okay. It's just water."

She sniffled and watched him as she seemed to think it over for a minute or two. Then, apparently the crisis passed, because she smiled and patted his face.

God. She already had a hold on him with those tiny fingers of hers. His heart did another slow tumble and Reed told himself to be careful. To not be drawn in so deeply he wouldn't be able to defend himself. Maybe the answer here was to show Lilah he could and would care for Rose, but to hold enough of himself back that he wouldn't eventually have his heart crushed.

He stood in the bathroom, looked into the mirror and saw his own rumpled reflection, holding a tiny wet baby. Bath time should definitely prove to Lilah that he was willing to involve himself with Rose, right? And that was good, wasn't it? Lilah would leave when he and Rose had "bonded" and then he could get back to the way life should be lived without constantly thinking about a woman he shouldn't be thinking about.

Reed wondered if he was losing his mind. His sharp, cagey brain was fogged a lot lately and he had the feeling it was all because of Lilah. Desire was eating away at his logic. *Bonded.*

"Stupid word, isn't it, Rose?"

"What's stupid?" Lilah spoke up from the doorway.

He groaned inwardly. See? Another example of foggy brain. He hadn't even heard Lilah approach. Shaking his head a little, he met her gaze in the mirror. She looked good, of course. Even in faded jeans and a pale blue T-shirt, Lilah Strong was enough to make a man's mouth water. No wonder he was foggy. With her around, he would challenge *any* guy to keep his mind on the mundane. Not like he could tell her that, though. So he did the first thing he could think of and lied.

"Nothing. Rose was just telling me she thought USC would beat UCLA this fall and I told her that was stupid. Nobody beats the Bruins."

"Uh-huh." Lilah's fabulous mouth curved. "Big football fan, is she?"

"Who isn't?"

She studied him and he realized he could get lost in those blue eyes of hers. The color of summer skies, or clear lakes. Her red-gold hair was a constant fascination to him, and now that he'd had his hands in that heavy, silky mass, all he could think about was doing it again. Her lips were full and shaped into a slight smile that made a single dimple wink in her cheek, and all he could think about was getting another taste of that mouth.

He was in deep trouble here, and when he took a breath and dragged the scent of lilacs into his lungs, he almost groaned aloud. Seriously, couldn't the woman pick *one* scent and stick to it? The changeup was making him crazy.

"Are you okay?" she asked.

"What? Yeah. Fine." Perfect. His poker face had almost completely dissolved now. Somehow, this one woman managed to always keep him off guard—which was another good reason for her to get back to her own life as soon as possible and leave him to his. "Did you want something?"

"Just to tell you your sister Savannah's here."

"Here?"

"*Right* here, actually." Savannah stepped up behind Lilah and grinned.

The huge master bath was beginning to feel like a broom closet.

"Well," Savannah said, still smiling, "here's something I never thought I'd see. Reed Hudson bathing a baby."

He sighed at his sister's teasing. Savannah's short black hair hugged her scalp and her eyes were the same shade of green as his own. He, Savannah and their brother James were the first batch of Hudson siblings, and they were all close.

Though he was surprised to see Savannah, he shouldn't have been. A few days ago, Reed had sent out an email blast to the entire family giving them his new address. It had been only a matter of time before they started trickling in to see him, demanding help with one thing or another.

"What's up, Savannah?" He kept his gaze on his sister, since she was far too observant, and if he chanced glancing at Lilah, his sister would no doubt see more than he wanted her to. He was less and less sure of his ability to mask his thoughts since Lilah had entered his life. After all, if she could read him after knowing each other only two weeks, his sister would probably be able to pick thoughts right from his brain.

"Nothing much." Savannah lifted one shoulder in a shrug. "Just wanted to see your new place, see Spring's baby and—"

*"And?"* He waited, knowing there was a real reason for her visit. None of the siblings came by or called unless they needed something.

"Okay," she said with a laugh, "I want to use the family jet and the pilot won't take off without your say-so."

He frowned. "Where are you going?"

"Just Paris for a week or two. I need a change," she said and gave him the pout that had always worked on their father. It didn't have the same effect on Reed, because he knew she used that poor-little-me look as her most effective weapon. "I broke up with Sean and I need some me time. You know how it is, right?"

The last, she directed at Lilah, who had been watching the byplay silently. "Um…"

When she got no support from Lilah, Savannah turned back to her brother. "Come on, Reed. Be a sport. You're not using it in the next day or two, are you?"

"No," he said, jiggling the baby a little when she began to squirm.

"So what's the problem?" Savannah turned and said, "Lilah, right? You're with me on this, aren't you? I mean, you know what it feels like to just need a break, right?"

Lilah smiled and shook her head. "I don't know. When I take a break from work, I drive to the city. I've never been to Paris."

"Oh, my God." Savannah looked at her as if Lilah had confessed to being a serial killer. "Seriously? You've *got* to go. Make Reed take you. Well, after my trip," she added quickly. "But you should definitely go. There is this amazing little street café right near Sacré-Coeur…"

While his sister babbled on about the wonders of the City of Lights, Reed jiggled the baby nestled against him, trying to keep her happy. That's when he felt a sudden warmth spread across his chest.

"Oh, man." He looked down at the naked baby in his arms and realized he really should have put a diaper on her right away.

"What's wrong?" Lilah asked instantly.

"Nothing," Reed muttered. "She just—"

Picking up on what had happened, Savannah laughed in delight. "She peed on you! God, Spring would have laughed so hard right now…"

As soon as she said it, silence settled over the three of them like a cold blanket. In the harsh bathroom light, Reed could see the signs of grieving that his sister had tried to conceal with a bright smile. Even as he watched her, Savannah sobered and she looked from Reed to Lilah. Shaking her head, she swallowed hard, blew out a breath and whispered, "I can't believe she's gone. Not really, you know?"

"I feel the same way," Lilah said softly, reaching out one hand to lay it on Savannah's arm. "Spring was a good friend to me, but she was your sister and I'm so sorry."

Lost in the face of his sister's pain, Reed was grateful for the sympathy in Lilah's gaze and voice. Helping Savannah or any of the others deal with Spring's death was especially hard for him since he hadn't actually dealt with it yet himself.

"That's why you really want to go to Paris, isn't it?" Reed asked.

"Yes," Savannah admitted on a sigh. "Sean was just another ship in the night, but Spring…" She winced a little. "We went to Paris together five years ago, remember?"

Reed gave her a tired smile and said wryly, "I remember getting a late-night call from a gendarme asking me if I was willing to pay bail for you and Spring after you went swimming in a public fountain."

Savannah laughed and lifted one hand to cover her mouth. "That's right. I'd forgotten about that. God, we had fun on that trip. Now… I just want to go back. Remember."

Reed looked into her eyes and saw the misery just beneath the surface and he understood her need to go back, retrace her steps with their lost sister. Try to relive the joy to ease the pain. Though none of their parents would win any awards for their skills at nurturing, all of the siblings had managed to stay close.

He had no doubt that Savannah was thinking of a trip to Paris as a sort of wake for the sister she would miss so much. Hell, he knew how she felt. He felt it, too. Here he stood, holding his sister's child, and the baby girl would never remember her mother. Reed would never see Spring again. Never hear that raucous laugh of hers, and it tore at him that the last time he'd seen her, they'd parted angrily. He'd never get that moment back. Never be able to rewrite the past.

Too many *nevers*, he told himself. Too much left unsaid, undone, and now, too late to change a damn thing.

"If it helps to know it," Lilah was saying, her voice breaking through his thoughts, "Spring was really happy with her life. She had a lot of friends."

Savannah looked at Lilah for a long minute, then finally nodded. "It does help. Thank you. And you should know that whenever I talked to my sister, she told me about how kind you were. How much she loved her job."

Now Reed was surprised. Savannah had known about Spring actually working? Was he the only one his sister hadn't confided in?

Turning to her brother again, Savannah said, "I'm so glad I came here in person instead of calling. I like seeing you with the baby and I think Spring would get a real kick out of it, too."

"Yeah," Reed said, still holding the squirmy, wet baby close to his chest. "You're right. She would."

He looked from the baby to Savannah to Lilah and realized that he was surrounded by women—and that wasn't even counting Connie, who was off in the kitchen. Yeah, Spring would have loved seeing him like this. And the thought made him smile.

How his life had changed in a couple of short weeks.

"So?" his sister prodded. "Can I use the plane?"

Nodding, he said, "I'll call the pilot. Let him know you're coming."

Lilah looked up at him, gave him a wide, approving smile, and for some reason, Reed felt as if he'd just won a medal.

"Savannah seemed nice," Lilah said later as she shared tea and some of Connie's magic chocolate chip bars with the housekeeper in the kitchen.

And, she thought as she took another bite and gave an inner sigh, Reed was right. They were "magic."

Lilah loved this room. As with any house, the kitchen really was the heart of things. And this one was amazing. It could have graced the pages of any magazine. The walls were cream colored, the miles of quartz counter were white with streaks of gray marbling. Upper cabinets were white, lowers were a dark gray and the floor was a wide-plank dark walnut. Tucked into the nook where a bay window offered a view of the backyard, the two women sat at an oak pedestal table. A silver pendant light that looked like an old-fashioned gas lamp hung over the table and provided the only light in the otherwise darkened room.

"Oh," Connie said with a laugh, "that Savannah has a good soul but a wild heart. She's always up to something." Chuckling now, she added, "Always had a plan cooking in that quick brain of hers. She spent many a night in my kitchen washing dishes for some transgression or other."

Lilah smiled in response. "Reed told me that you were their real parent."

Flushing with pleasure, Connie shook her head, took a sip of tea and said, "Not really, but I'm sure it felt that way to them from time to time. Anyway, it was good to see Savannah even though it was a quick visit."

Quick indeed. Reed's sister had left almost immediately after he'd called the airport to okay her flight to Paris. As for Reed, once he'd dressed Rose in her pj's and got her into bed, he'd shut himself up in his study. He hadn't so much as poked his head out in hours.

And Lilah had had to force herself to leave him to his solitude. But there'd been a look on his face when

Savannah had rushed out—as if he wished she'd stayed longer. But he hadn't said anything. Hadn't asked her to sit down for a while and have a cup of coffee, and she wondered why. It was as if the distance he tried to keep with Rose was simply the way he treated everyone he cared about.

Had he always been so closed off? Or was it a self-defense mechanism? And if it was, what was he protecting himself from? She had more questions than answers and Lilah knew there was one sure way to get some insight into who exactly Reed Hudson was. Talk to the woman who'd raised him.

"Reed didn't seem surprised to have his sister dash in and out."

"Oh," Connie said, taking a sip of tea, "he's used to that. All of the siblings come and go from his life regularly." She set her cup down and continued, "They love each other, but every last one of them has a *loner* streak. I suppose that's to be expected, since their parents really did leave them to their own devices more often than not. And, ever since he was a teenager, the others have turned to Reed to solve problems."

Lilah's heart ached a little for the loneliness he must have felt as a child. Lilah's own childhood had been great. With two parents who loved each other and doted on her, she'd never been left on her own.

"But he was just a kid, too."

Connie laughed a little. "I think Reed was born old. At least, he has an old soul. Never a single day's trouble out of that boy. Always did what was expected of him, never made waves. He had his own...*code*, I guess you'd say. His own rules for living, even as a little boy. To tell the truth, I used to wish he would rebel a little. But he's always had the maturity that the rest of the family—" she broke off and scowled "—including his parents, lacked."

Now Lilah had the mental image of a little boy, carving out a set of rules so he could keep the world around him safe. Was that what his private wall was about? Keeping out people who might disturb his sense of order?

"Really?" Lilah had already realized that a one-word question would be enough to keep Connie talking.

"Oh, don't get me wrong," Connie said, and the halo of light from the pendant fixture overhead gilded her hair and shone in her eyes. "His parents aren't evil by any means. They love the kids, they're just…careless. Careless with what means the most and the sad thing is, they won't realize it until it's too late to change anything.

"One day they'll be old and wondering why their children don't come to visit." She nodded to herself and gave a little sigh. "They've no real relationship with their own children and that's a sad statement to make, I think."

"It is," Lilah agreed. She couldn't imagine the kind of childhood Reed and his siblings had had. But it still didn't give her insight into the man. And she found she wanted to know him.

"Does he see a lot of his family?"

"Well, now," Connie admitted, "I've not had a chance to see it on a daily basis for the last couple of years. But when the kids come to visit me, they often talk of Reed."

"They visit you?"

"Sure they do," Connie said, laughing. "I'm the one who smacked their bottoms, dried their tears and took care of them when they were sick, aren't I?"

His parents might not have been worth much, Lilah thought, but he'd had Connie and somehow that made her feel much better both about his childhood and Rose's situation, as well. With Connie in her life, Rosie would get plenty of affection and care, Lilah told herself.

"Reed's told me how much you meant to all of them. To *him*."

Connie smiled, clearly pleased to hear it. "They're all good people, every last one of them. And I know how they'll all miss Spring." She took a breath and slowly turned her teacup on the counter in tiny circles. "But I think it will hit Reed hardest—once he finally allows himself the chance to mourn her. He was always the one who took charge of the others. And losing her hurt him. I can see it in him."

"I can, too," Lilah mused. More tonight than ever before. It was seeing him with Savannah, she thought. The brother and sister having that sorrow-filled moment over their sister. While Savannah's pain had been obvious to anyone looking at her, seeing that same anguish in Reed took more effort. But Lilah had seen his brilliant green eyes go momentarily soft and she'd read the regret in those depths. Her heart hurt for him and she was surprised by the strength of her compassion.

When she'd arrived here, she'd expected to hate him on sight. To resent him for taking Rose away from her. Now she was beginning to feel for him, understand what drove him.

"The others now," Connie said after a moment, "they come and go from Reed's life. Each of them will pop in from time to time, usually when they need something, then they disappear again until there's a new need. He'd never say it, but I imagine that bothers him."

"It would bother anyone," Lilah said and she found herself offended on his behalf. Did his siblings appreciate him only for what he could do for them?

"Reed's a strong one. He's made himself so." Connie lifted her cup for a sip. "But there's a fine line, I think, between being strong and being hard. I worry that he doesn't see it."

So did Lilah. The wall he'd built around himself was so solid, she had thought it impenetrable. But there had been one or two times when she'd sensed a chink in his armor.

"Well," Connie announced, "morning comes early, so I'm off to bed. Just leave the teacups here on the table, Lilah. I'll take care of them in the morning."

"Okay. Good night." She watched Connie walk to her suite and for a minute, Lilah just sat there in the kitchen, listening to the silence. The refrigerator hummed and ice thunked into the bin. She checked the time and told herself to go to bed. It was already eleven o'clock and Connie was right, morning would come early. Rosie wasn't one for sleeping in.

But Lilah wasn't ready for bed. She felt…restless.

She stood, then turned the lights off, plunging the room into darkness as she left and headed down the hall. Her mind was busy, rehashing that scene with Savannah, then the conversation with Connie. Which turned her thoughts to Reed. No surprise there, since he'd spent a lot of time front and center in her brain over the past couple of weeks.

But now, along with the attraction she'd felt from the start, there was also…admiration and a tug of—not sympathy, she assured herself. He didn't need her pity and wouldn't want it even if he did. But she could feel bad for him that his family came to him only when they needed something from him.

The more she thought about him, the more she wanted

to see him. Talk to him. Assure herself he was okay and not sitting in a dark room feeling sad or depressed or... Oh, hell, she just wanted to see him. Before she could talk herself out of it, Lilah marched up to the closed study door and knocked.

# Seven

"What is it?"

He didn't sound happy and Lilah almost changed her mind, but then she remembered that look in his eyes when he and Savannah were remembering Spring. Nope, she wasn't going to leave him alone until she knew he was all right.

She opened the door, poked her head inside and asked, "Are you busy?"

She could see he wasn't. The room was dark, but firelight spilled out into the shadows, creating weird images that danced across the ceiling and walls.

Rather than sitting behind his desk, he was on the other side of the room in one of the wide leather chairs pulled up in front of the wide, stone hearth, facing the fire. Those shadows moved over his features as he half turned to look at her. There was a short glass of what she guessed was scotch sitting on the table beside him.

She noted his usually tidy hair looked as if he'd been stabbing his fingers through it repeatedly. He wore a short-sleeved black T-shirt that he'd changed into after bathing Rose and a pair of worn jeans that looked as good on him as his usual uniform of elegant suits. He was barefoot, legs kicked out in front of him, and again, she had to wonder what it was about bare feet that had become so sexy all of a sudden.

"Good, I'm glad you're not busy," she said, walking over to sit down in the chair beside his.

He scowled at her. "Who said I wasn't?"

"I did. You're having a drink and staring at a fire. That's not busy. That's brooding."

"I'm not brooding," he argued. "I'm busy thinking."

"About?"

His scowl deepened and, weirdly, Lilah found it sort of cute. He probably thought it was intimidating, but he was wrong. At least, as far as Lilah was concerned.

"You're damn nosy," he mused, gaze fixed on her.

"If you're not, you never find out anything," she argued, then picked up his glass and took a sip. Instantly the fire of the expensive liquor burned a line down her throat and settled into her stomach to smolder.

"Please," he said, waving one hand. "Help yourself."

"No thanks, one sip of that is plenty. How do you stand it?" Firelight danced in his eyes and shadows chased each other across his features.

Smirking a little, he said, "Hundred-year-old scotch is an acquired taste. I acquired it."

He was probably hoping that if he was surly enough, she'd leave. But wrong again. She glanced around the room, pleased with how it had turned out. There were bookcases behind his desk and along one wall, with paintings and framed awards hanging on the opposite wall. The stone hearth took up a third side of the room, while floor-to-ceiling windows made up the fourth. It was male, but cozy.

"Your sister seems nice."

He snorted and picked up his glass for another sip. "Savannah is a force of nature. Like a hurricane. They're rarely nice."

Lilah saw more than she suspected he wanted her to see. He loved his sister, that had been clear. And though he sounded dismissive now, he was just doing the whole don't-get-too-close thing. "Do you see her often?"

He slanted her a look. "Writing a book?"

"Keeping secrets?" she countered, smiling to take the sting out of her accusation.

He sighed, turned his gaze back to the fire and said, "She drops in from time to time."

"When she needs something?" Lilah asked, wanting to see his reaction.

"Usually." Frowning, he turned his gaze back to her. "Why do you care? And why are you asking so many questions?"

"Like I said, if you want answers, you have to ask questions." She ran her fingers over the edge of the table. "I just wondered if you and your brothers and sisters see much of each other."

His brow furrowed, he asked, "Why does that matter?"

She couldn't very well tell him that she was worried that his siblings were taking advantage of him, so she lied instead. "I want to know if Rose will have lots of aunts and uncles coming over all the time."

He took another sip of scotch and drained the glass. "I told you I'd take care of her."

"I'm not arguing that," she said, and wished she'd come up with a better lie. She hadn't come in here to argue with him. She'd wanted to...talk. To make sure he was okay. And that sounded just pitiful, even to her.

"Well, that's a first." Reed pushed to his feet, walked to the wet bar in the corner and refilled his glass. "You've been arguing with me since the first day I met you."

She supposed that was true, but their *relationship*, if that was what it was, hadn't exactly started out friendly, had it?

"To be fair," she said, standing up to walk to him, "you did a lot of that, too."

He studied her through eyes that suddenly looked as dark and mysterious as a forest at midnight, and something fluttered into life inside her. What was it about Reed Hudson that turned her insides to jelly and made her want to both argue and comfort at the same time? Lilah took a breath and steadied herself, for all the good it would do. Being this close to him, having his eyes pinned on her, was enough to unsettle any woman's balance.

"And now what?" he asked. "We're friends?"

"We could be," she said, though a part of her doubted it. There was too much underlying tension simmering between them for a friendship. She didn't have any other "friend" she imagined naked.

"We won't be," he said and set his glass down with a click.

He turned to face her and Lilah's stomach did a slow spin as her heart gave one hard lurch. Nerves jangled into life inside her, but she paid no attention. The night was late, the room was dark but for firelight simmering in the shadows. There was closeness here and she didn't want it to end.

*Stupid*, her brain warned and Lilah didn't listen. She didn't want to think too much about what was going on between them right now, because she didn't want this quiet, intimate moment to end. Not yet. "Why not, Reed?"

"Because I don't want to be your *friend*, Lilah. What I want from you has nothing to do with being pals."

She took another breath, but it didn't help. Her balance was dissolving and she didn't care. Staring into those green eyes of his was mesmerizing. She couldn't have looked away if she had tried. And she didn't want to try. Lilah wanted to look into his eyes until she discovered everything about him. Until the wall he hid behind fell crashing to the ground.

"My friends don't smell as good as you do," he said quietly. "They don't have hair that looks like gold and feels like silk."

Lilah shivered. She'd known when she knocked on the study door that *this* was what she had been heading toward. For two weeks now, her mind had been filled with nothing but thoughts of Reed Hudson. Even her dreams had been pushing her here, to this moment in the darkness with him.

"What if I don't want to be your friend, either?" she whispered.

"Then I'd say we're wasting precious time standing here talking," Reed said, moving in on her, "when we could be doing something far more interesting."

Awareness roared to life inside her and Lilah felt every single cell in her body wake up and jostle each other with eagerness. She gave him a slow smile that belied the nerves boiling in the pit of her stomach. "Is that right?"

He stepped up so close, their shirts brushed against each other. She felt heat pumping from his body and knew that her own was sizzling, too. Bending his head toward her, he inhaled sharply and murmured, "Vanilla today. I like it."

"Show me," she said and met his mouth in a kiss that lit up every inch of her body. Just like the first time he kissed her, spontaneous explosions of desire, need, hunger were set off inside her, one after the other. She was rocked by the force of them, stronger than before, as if her body had just been waiting, biding its time until it could finally let loose.

He pulled her in tight against him, his hands running up and down her spine, curving over her bottom, holding her close enough she couldn't miss his body's reaction to the kiss. And knowing that he felt the same throbbing need she did only fed the fires licking at the edges of her soul.

The core of her throbbed and pulsed in time with the beat of her heart that was so fast it left her nearly breathless. But then, she thought wildly, who needed air?

He didn't let her go as he moved forward, with Lilah backing up until she bumped into the edge of his desk. Their mouths still fused together, Lilah's tongue tangled with his as he swept inside her mouth to explore, to taste, to torture.

It had been a long time since she'd been with a man and even then, she'd felt nothing close to what she experienced with Reed. This was something brand new. Exciting. Amazing. The man had talented hands and his mouth was downright lethal.

He suddenly tore that mouth from hers and dropped his head to the curve of her neck. His lips, tongue and teeth made a trail along the length of her throat and Lilah groaned as she tipped her head to one side, giving him better access. Silently asking for *more*.

As if he heard her, he lifted both hands to cup her breasts and even through the fabric of her shirt and the lace bra beneath, she felt the heat of him. Her nipples pebbled and every stroke of his fingers sent a shooting star of sensation slicing through her. She gasped, letting her head fall back as her breath whipped in and out of her lungs. Staring at the ceiling, she blindly watched the fire-lit shadows shifting, pulsing in the darkness.

All she felt was him. Every last, hard inch of him pressing her into the edge of the desk. His muscular thighs aligned with hers and she held on to his waist to keep from falling. She wanted him on her, in her, over her. She wanted to feel his body pushing into hers, and easing the ache that only seemed to grow more frantic with every passing second.

He was tall and strong and really built. That one wild thought careened through her mind even as his fingers began to tug at the buttons of her blouse. Impatient now, for the feel of his hands on her skin, she tried to help, but only fumbled and got in his way.

"I've got it," he whispered harshly, his voice straining over every word. "Don't help."

"Right, right." She nodded, grateful he could still move since she seemed to be nearly paralyzed with her body's insistent demands, which clutched in her chest, her gut and, oh, so much lower.

Then he had her blouse undone and was pushing it off, down her arms to land on the desk behind her. The air in the room was cool in spite of the fire and she shivered a little. But then his hands were back on her breasts and heat spiraled up out of nowhere, delivering a different kind of shiver.

His nimble fingers flicked the front clasp of her bra and then her breasts were free and being cupped and stroked by those amazing hands of his. His thumbs and forefingers circled her nipples, tugging, pulling gently. He kissed her again, a sweep of his tongue across her lips, as if offering her a small taste of something incredible.

"Oh, boy," she said on a sigh and caught his satisfied smile.

"Only getting better from here," he promised, and Lilah could hardly wait. She'd never been like this before, her mind whispered. Never felt so much, wanted so much. No man before him had emptied her brain and filled her body so quickly, so completely.

At the core of her, she trembled and ached, and dampness filled the heat at her center. She was more than ready for whatever would come next and she let him know just how eager she was, by reaching up, cupping his face in her palms and dragging his mouth to hers.

Again and again, they claimed each other, breath sliding from one to the other as they delved into a pool of unbelievable sensations. And still it wasn't enough. Not nearly.

She reached beneath the hem of his T-shirt and flattened her palms against the hard planes of his chest. She felt the definition of sculpted muscles and nearly whimpered with the glory of it.

He hissed in a breath, then ripped his shirt off before pulling her tight against him again. Skin to skin, heartbeat to heartbeat, they clung together, relishing every brush of their bodies as the flames around them flashed higher, stronger.

"That's it," he said thickly. "We're done here."

"What? *What?*" She shook her head. Was he stopping? Was he going to say good-night and leave her like this? Needy? Desperate?

"My room," he said shortly, snatching up her blouse and laying it around her shoulders. "We're going to my room. To a bed."

Lowering as it was to admit, she didn't want to wait that long. Oh, she was in serious trouble. "Don't need a bed."

"There're condoms in my room." He looked at her.

*Duh.* "Right. Of course. Do need those." She held on to her blouse with one hand as he grabbed her other hand and tugged her in his wake. They left the shadow-filled room and walked down a darkened hallway, following the dimly lit path provided by the night-lights plugged into wall sockets. His long legs were hard to keep up with, but Lilah managed, driven by the growing hunger chewing at her.

He pulled her into his bedroom and the only light there came from the slant of moonlight streaming through the windows to lay like silver across his king-size bed. The navy blue comforter looked as wide and dark as the sky. And when he picked her up and dropped her onto it, she felt as if she was flying into that dark expanse.

Moonlight gleamed in his eyes as she stared up at him, and when she lifted her arms to him, he went to her, sliding his body up and along hers. The incredible brush of his skin felt electrifying. He kissed her again and she felt herself drowning in his taste, in the heat of him.

She tossed her blouse aside then shrugged out of her bra and tossed it, as well. Lilah didn't want anything coming between them. She wanted, needed, and she didn't want to wait. For the first time in her life, Lilah was spiraling out of control.

He grinned as if he knew what she was thinking and completely agreed. "Now the jeans," he muttered and reached for the snap on her pants, but Lilah was too fast for him. She had them undone in a blink and then he was sliding them and her panties down off her legs.

If she was thinking right now, she might have felt a little embarrassed, uneasy, being naked in his bed, the cool night air kissing her skin, the fire in his eyes warming her. But she didn't want to think. She only wanted to *feel*.

"Now you," she demanded and wasn't willing to be patient about it, either. It had been a long two weeks, Lilah told herself, filled with bristling tension and heightened awareness until she'd hardly been able to sleep at night.

She kept her gaze on him while he quickly stripped, and she was really glad she did. He was beautiful. His broad chest was leanly sculpted muscle. Narrow hips, long legs and…her eyes widened and her heart gave an almost painful jolt in her chest. Oh, my.

He grinned again and Lilah said, "You have to stop reading my mind."

"But it's so interesting," he countered, joining her on the bed, dropping a kiss on her flat belly, then moving up to take first one nipple then the other into his mouth.

Lilah came up off the bed, digging her heels into the mattress as she arched her back, instinctively moving closer to that amazing, talented, wonderful mouth of his. She held his head to her breast and watched as his tongue drew lazy, sensual circles around her nipple.

"God, you taste good," he whispered against her breast, giving her skin another long lick.

"It's my soaps," she said on a sigh. "Organic. You could eat them if you wanted to."

"Your scent's been driving me crazy for two weeks," he admitted, looking at her briefly before slowly trailing his mouth down her body again. "Every night, I lay there wondering what you're going to smell like in the morning. Lemons?" Kiss. "Oranges?" Kiss. "Cinnamon?" Kiss.

And now he was close, so close to the throbbing, aching center of her. Everything in her clenched in anticipation, expectation. She held her breath as he shifted on the bed, as he moved to kneel between her legs. As he bent his head to—

"Oh!" Her hips rocked helplessly as his mouth covered her, as his tongue slipped over one sensitive nub of flesh. His hands squeezed her bottom, then moved over her body, sliding up to cup her breasts again, tweaking her nipples while his mouth worked her body into a frantic mass of raw nerves.

Lilah reached down, tangling her fingers in his hair, never wanting him to stop what he was doing—even though she wanted him inside her, filling her, easing the empty ache that hammered against her with every beat of her heart.

His tongue stroked, caressed, his breath dusted her skin and she moved with him, chasing the building need, trying to ease it, trying to make it last at the same time. Tension coiled, tightened until every breath was a victory. Her mind fogged over, her body took charge, racing toward the completion that remained just out of reach.

He pushed her higher, faster, never letting the pressure ease. She both loved and hated him for it. Her head whipped from side to side on the mattress. Her hips continued to move against him. She had no control, wanted none. All she wanted was... The first ripple began and Lilah braced for what was coming.

But there was simply no way she could have prepared herself for the conflagration that erupted inside her. Her head tipped back, her eyes closed and her body bucked and shivered as he sent her flailing over the edge of reality into a skyrocket-filled fantasy.

"Reed... Reed..." She gasped for air and groaned his name, when he moved away from her. But while the last of the tremors were still rippling through her, she heard a drawer open and snap closed.

Moments later, Reed covered her body with his and thrust himself deep inside her. Lilah gasped again at the absolute completeness she felt. He was big and strong and his body felt as if it was meant to be a part of hers.

"You're beautiful," he whispered. "I love watching you shatter."

She choked out a laugh followed by a gasp as he thrust deeply inside her. "Then pay attention, it's about to happen again."

Chuckling, Reed dipped his head to her mouth and tangled his tongue with hers. He stroked one hand along her body, up and down and then back up to cover her breast as he moved in and out of her with a wild, possessive rhythm that stole her breath and made sure she didn't care.

Lilah's legs came up, wrapped around his hips and clung there as her hands grasped his shoulders, nails digging into his skin. Again and again, he took her breath away. Staring up into his emerald green eyes, she lost what was left of her sanity. All she knew was the feel of him moving within her, the brilliant stab of his gaze and the delicious friction of his skin moving against hers.

And then the tension coiled in her belly suddenly spilled throughout her system. She rushed to meet what she knew was coming. Moving with him, rushing together toward that pinnacle, she cried out his name as new, fresh waves of pleasure washed through her. And while her brain fogged over, she heard him groan, felt his body tremble and Lilah held him as they both fell from the sky.

What could have been minutes or hours later, Lilah stirred halfheartedly. She was content right where she was, with Reed's body pressing her into the mattress. But her legs had lost all feeling—unless it was hysterical paralysis.

She wouldn't have been surprised.

Reed Hudson was something she never could have prepared for. He was, in a word, astonishing. She shifted a little beneath him and stroked one hand down his back.

"I'm squashing you."

"Are you?" she asked, a smile of pure female satisfaction curving her lips. It was a powerful thing for a woman to bring a strong man to such a state that he couldn't move. "I hadn't noticed."

Rather than reply, he rolled to one side, but kept her with him, dragging her on top of him. "Better," he said.

Since she could breathe now, she had to agree. Smoothing his hair back from his forehead, she said, "Well, that was worth waiting for."

"Yeah." He looked into her eyes. "I guess it was."

Idly, he traced his hand down her back to her behind and caressed her in long, lazy strokes.

When he closed his eyes and simply let his arm lay across her waist, Lilah took the chance to study him. Always when they talked, when they were even in the same room together, he maintained a closed expression and wariness in his eyes. Seeing him like this, unguarded, tugged at her heart.

But the minute that thought entered her mind, she discounted it. This had been about lust, not love. There were no hearts involved here and if she was smart, she'd keep it that way.

As spectacular as their little interlude had been, it hadn't really changed a darn thing. If anything, she'd only complicated matters by sleeping with him. Not that it hadn't been worth it, but Lilah was a big believer in never making the same mistake twice. So as much as she hated it, there couldn't be a repeat performance and now was as good a time as any to break the news.

"Reed..."

He didn't answer, and she frowned. "Reed."

Still nothing. Stunned, Lilah realized that while she had been doing some soul-searching and coming to a hard, but reasonable conclusion... Reed had fallen asleep.

"Well, I guess our little talk will have to wait, won't it?" Shaking her head, she rolled off him, stretched out on the bed and turned her head on the pillow to look at him. He didn't look young and innocent in his sleep. He looked exactly what he was... A strong, powerful man at rest. And for some ridiculous reason, she felt another hard tug on her heart. Oh, Lilah thought, that was probably not a good thing.

Easing out of the bed, she picked up her discarded clothes and left his room. But on the threshold, she couldn't resist glancing over her shoulder for one last look at him.

He slept in the moonlight and looked so alone, she almost went back to him. Almost. Before she could give in to an urge she would only come to regret, she stepped out of the room and carefully closed the door behind her.

By morning, Reed had worked out exactly what he would say to Lilah. He figured that she would be just like every other woman he'd ever encountered—assuming that sex was a natural gateway to a "relationship." Not going to happen.

Naturally, though, Lilah had thrown him for a loop again. Not only hadn't they had "the talk," she hadn't even been home by the time he walked into the kitchen looking for coffee. Connie had explained that Lilah had taken Rose for an early morning walk and he'd had to tell himself that talking to her about what had happened the night before would just have to wait until he got home after work.

Home. The house was quickly becoming home. More of Lilah's influence. She'd furnished it so that every time he stepped inside, he relaxed as he never had in the impersonal, starkly modern hotel. Hell, he'd even been thinking about redecorating the office lately because he didn't like all the chrome and black.

Her influence.

She was seeping into every corner of his life—and he knew he'd never be able to sleep in his bed again without remembering what the two of them had shared there.

Okay, yes, it had been the most incredible experience of his life, but that didn't mean anything, really. Of course sex with Lilah had been mind-blowing. He'd done nothing but think about and fantasize about her for the past couple of weeks. Finally getting her into his bed was...staggering. Okay, fine, he could admit the sex was great. But that didn't mean he was interested in anything more.

He had spent a lifetime building a controlled, organized life. With his extended, wildly passionate family, he'd learned to maintain a certain emotional distance. Mainly because if he allowed himself to be drawn into every crisis his family brought to him to solve, his own life would end up as convoluted as those he worked to keep out of trouble.

So control had been a part of his personality for as far back as he could remember. Reed kept his thoughts and emotions to himself and showed the world only what he wanted them to see. That control had allowed him to build a fortune, a career and a reputation he was proud of and to avoid messy entanglements like the rest of his family.

But since Rose and Lilah had walked into his life, that control had been slipping. He didn't like it, but there was no point in lying to himself about it.

The truth was, Rosie had already wedged her way into his heart. That tiny girl had a grip on him he wouldn't have thought possible. Then there was Lilah.

He sat back in his desk chair, spun it around to look out at the sun-splashed ocean and instead of seeing the Pacific, he saw Lilah. Her eyes. Her hair. Her smile. He saw her tending to Rose, laughing with Connie and sitting beside him in the firelight.

But damn it, mostly he saw her in his bed. Naked,

writhing, calling his name as her body erupted beneath his.

Before Lilah Strong, his life had rolled along as it should. Okay, maybe it had its boring moments... Fine. He was bored. Work didn't hold the same appeal it had years before. Reed watched his brothers and sisters having adventures and, yes, screwing up so he had to ride to the rescue, but still. They were *living*.

While he, like an old man at a party, complained about the crowds, the noise and the irritations.

When had he turned into an old fogy?

"I'm not," he muttered, as if he'd needed to hear it said out loud for it to be true. "I can have a good time. I just choose to live my life responsibly."

Groaning at the thought, he frowned at the buzzer on his phone when it sounded. Stabbing the button, he asked, "What is it, Karen?"

"Ms. Strong is on the phone. She insists on talking to you."

Just thinking about her could conjure her—if not in person, then on the phone. Well, hell, maybe "the talk" they should have had that morning would be easier if they had it on the phone. He wasn't looking forward to it. She'd probably cry, tell him she loved him or some such thing. But he'd be cool. Detached. And set her straight. "Fine. Put her through."

"Reed?" Her voice sounded low and worried and instantly he responded.

"Are you okay? Rose? Connie?"

"Everything's fine," she whispered. "I don't like bothering you at work, but—"

Thoughts of "the talk" had faded from his mind. Now

all he could think about was what must have happened at the house to have Lilah calling him.

"What's going on?"

"There's a little boy here."

"What?"

"A little boy? Male child?" Even whispered, he caught the sarcasm. "He says he's your brother Micah."

Reed jumped to his feet. "Micah's there? He's supposed to be in school."

"Well, he's in the kitchen eating everything Connie puts in front of him and he says he'll only talk to you."

"I'm on my way." He hung up, grabbed his suit jacket and on the way out the door could only wonder when he would have the time to be bored again.

# Eight

Lilah liked Micah Hudson.

He was twelve years old, had Reed's green eyes and a shock of dark hair that continually fell into those eyes. He also had quite the appetite. He'd already mowed through two sandwiches, a half a bag of chips, three of Connie's chocolate chip bars and three glasses of milk.

And through it all, he managed to maintain a guarded look in his eyes that she'd noticed in Reed's way too often. Lilah thought no child should look so wary and it tore at her to see him sitting there waiting for the proverbial ax to fall.

"Reed's on his way home," she said as she sat down at the kitchen table opposite the boy.

"Okay, good." Micah looked up at her and bit down on his bottom lip. "Did he sound mad?"

"No," she assured him. Surprised, yes. Angry, no.

She'd seen Reed in action dealing with his sister Savannah, so she hoped he was just as understanding and patient with this boy who looked so worried and anxious. "He did say you're supposed to be in school."

Instantly, Micah slumped in the chair until he looked boneless. His head hung down so that his chin hit his chest and he muttered, "I don't want to be there. I wanted to come see Spring's baby." He looked at Rose, who gave him a wide, drooly smile, and Micah couldn't help but smile back. That expression faded when he looked back to Lilah. "They wouldn't let me come. Said my father had to sign a paper to *allow* me to go and he wouldn't."

For a boy who had at first insisted he'd speak only to his brother, once Micah started, he couldn't seem to stop. He picked up another cookie bar but instead of eating it, he crumbled it between his fingers as words poured from him in a flood.

"I called Father to tell him I wanted to come here but he said I couldn't come and see the baby because I had to stay at the school and be *supervised*." He added about six syllables to that last word for emphasis, then kept right on talking, his eyes flashing, and a stubborn expression settling on his features. "But Spring was my *sister*," he argued, eyes filling with tears he blinked back. "She *loved* me and I loved her. And now she's *dead*. I should get to see Rose, right?"

"I would think so," Lilah hedged, on his side, but wary about criticizing his father. That didn't keep her from reaching out to briefly lay one hand over his clenched fist.

"That's what I thought," Micah said, nodding as if to remind himself he'd done the right thing. "So, I had some money and I walked out of the school and bought a bus ticket and here I am."

She couldn't imagine a child just hopping a bus and taking off on his own. "Where do you go to school?"

"Arizona," he muttered and watched as cookie crumbs drifted like brown snow down to the plate in front of him. "And it sucks."

Arizona to California was a long bus ride for a little boy on his own, and Lilah took one silent moment to thank the universe for protecting him on his journey. Now that he was safe, Lilah could admire the courage it must have taken for him to go off on his own, and still, his eyes looked wounded, nervous.

Once again, Lilah was reminded of just how idyllic her own childhood had been. She'd never been forced to run away because she'd been miserable where she was. She'd never once gone to her parents with something important only to be turned away and ordered to basically sit down and shut up. She thought of what Connie had said about the Hudson parents and had to agree.

They were careless about the important things. Their children. Couldn't Micah's father hear the misery in the boy's voice? Had he even taken the time to help the boy grieve for his sister?

Oh, she really hoped Reed was kind when he showed up to talk to his younger brother. Micah didn't look as though he could take another dismissal of his feelings. But until Reed arrived, Lilah could only keep the boy talking, try to ease his fear and help him relax.

"Don't like Arizona, huh?" Lilah asked the question lightly, not letting him know how horrified she was that he'd taken such a chance by running. She handed Rosie a slice of banana that the tiny girl immediately squished in one small fist.

"It's not Arizona I don't like. It's my stupid school," Micah muttered.

He looked caught between childhood and adulthood. His face was still round and soft and would hone down over the years, making him a handsome man one day. But right now, he looked like a little boy, unsure of himself and the world around him. He wore black slacks, black shoes and a white shirt with a red-and-blue crest on the left pocket. The uniform had probably been starched and ironed when he began his trek. Now it looked as rumpled and stained as its wearer.

Lilah couldn't believe a twelve-year-old boy had just walked out of his private school and hopped on a bus. What kind of school was it that didn't keep better track of its students? And what kind of parent, she wondered again, couldn't see that a child was sick with worry and grief and misery? She felt sorry for the boy, but at the same time, she knew he'd been lucky to make the trip safely.

Rose, in a high chair alongside Micah, picked up a fistful of Cheerios and tossed them at the boy. Surprise flickered in Micah's eyes, then delight.

"I think she likes me," he said and his smile briefly chased the darkness from his eyes.

"Why wouldn't she?" Lilah told him, then stood up to answer the phone when it rang. Still smiling at the kids, she said, "Hudson residence."

"This is Robert Hudson speaking. Who are you?"

The gruff, hostile voice came through so loudly, Lilah lifted the receiver from her ear slightly. Reed's father? she wondered. "I'm Lilah Strong and I'm here to—"

"I know why you're there. You brought Spring's baby to Reed." There was a brief pause in that silence. Lilah heard a distinct tapping as if the man were slapping something against a tabletop in irritation. "Is my son Micah there?"

"Well," she hedged, not wanting to rat the boy out but unwilling to let his father worry any longer—if he *was* worried. She glanced at the boy, who was watching her through anxious eyes. "Yes, he is."

"I want to speak to him. Now. I've been handling phone calls from his school," he snapped, "and I knew damn well he'd make his way to Reed. I demand to speak to him now."

"Wow," she murmured and slid her gaze to where Micah sat, watching her. He had to have heard his father through the receiver. The man's furious voice was only getting louder. But as much as she wanted to shield Micah, she couldn't keep his father from talking to him. "Hold on, please." She cupped her hand over the phone and said, "It's your father."

Micah's smile was gone and his eyes looked haunted. Pushing himself out of his chair, he dragged himself across the floor like a man heading for the gallows, then reluctantly took the phone. "Hello, Father."

Instantly, the older Hudson started shouting even louder than before.

Lilah didn't mean to eavesdrop, but unless she actually left the room, she simply couldn't help it. She shot a worried glance at Connie and saw the older woman's scowl. But it was Micah's expression that tore at Lilah. As she watched, the boy seemed to shrink into himself as his father ranted like a crazy person.

A few words stood out from the stream. *Irresponsible. Brat. Selfish. Reckless.*

Lilah's temper simmered into a froth that nearly choked her. Seeing that sweet boy reduced to tears was just more than she was going to take.

"Give me the phone, Micah," she said.

The boy gaped at her, but handed it over. Lilah smiled at him, and ignoring the spiel pouring from the receiver, told the boy, "Why don't you go finish your cookies and sit with Rosie?"

He was looking at her wide-eyed as if he couldn't decide if she was brave or crazy. She was neither, Lilah thought. What she was, was going to defend a boy against a man who should know better than to rail against a child. He was still shouting.

"Mr. Hudson," Lilah spoke up and paused for the tirade to fade away in stunned shock at having been interrupted.

"Where's Micah?"

"He's having milk and cookies."

"Who the hell—"

She cut him off again and maybe it was small of her, but she enjoyed it. Now Lilah understood why Reed's siblings came to him when they had a problem. She couldn't imagine anyone would run to Robert Hudson for help. The man would no doubt throw a fit of humongous proportions and solve absolutely nothing.

Shaking her head, she had to admit she also had a whole new respect for what Reed had to deal with on a daily basis. Juggling so many different personalities had to be exhausting.

When Robert Hudson's voice finally trailed off, she spoke up.

"I'm sorry, but Micah's busy right now," she said and heard the man sputter on the other end of the phone. Smiling, she could silently admit that she sort of enjoyed knowing she'd thrown him for a loop. "But please call back as soon as you've had a chance to calm down."

"I beg your pardon?"

She almost smiled. "Goodbye, Mr. Hudson."

When she hung up the phone, Connie applauded. Lilah winced and laughed a little uneasily. Sure, the housekeeper might be pleased, but Lilah had just hung up on Reed's father. Not that she regretted it, she told herself when she looked at the boy staring at her with stars in his eyes. There was just no way she could have stood there and done nothing.

"That was so cool," Micah said quietly, awe coloring his tone. "Nobody but Reed talks to our father like that."

Hmm. "Well, maybe more people should."

Micah's gaze dropped and so did his voice. "Reed's gonna be mad at me, too, isn't he?"

Lilah really hoped not. She didn't think the boy could take much more right now. He looked beaten down after a few minutes of his father shouting at him. If Reed came in furious, it would only add to the boy's misery. Instantly, she thought back over the past couple of weeks and though she could remember a few times when Reed had behaved like a stuffy old man, she couldn't bring up one instance of him really being furious. And she had to admit, he'd had so many things thrown at him lately that he could have blown a gasket at any point. So maybe he'd be exactly what Micah needed.

"Reed will be happy to see you," Connie put in, stopping to give the boy a hard hug. "Just like I am."

"Thanks, Connie," he said, then shifted his gaze to

Lilah again. "Will you talk to Reed for me like you did to my father?"

She smiled and got him another glass of milk. That much at least, she could promise. "If you need it, sure."

"Okay." As settled as he could be, Micah focused on the baby and visibly tried to relax.

When Reed arrived a few minutes later, he came straight to the kitchen and Lilah's heart broke a little as she watched Micah straighten in his chair and go on guard. She really hoped Reed could see beyond the boy's bravado to the frightened kid inside.

Shrugging out of his jacket, Reed loosened his tie and glanced from Micah to the two women in the room watching him. Not for the first time, Lilah wished she could read his mind. It would be good to know if she'd have to jump in front of Micah or not.

But she told herself that how Reed treated his little brother would give her an idea of how he would deal with Rose in the years to come. Would he be patient or angry? Understanding or dictatorial? Nerves pinged inside her. She was sure there was a warm man beneath the cold, detached shell he showed the world. But what if she was wrong?

"Got any coffee, Connie?" he asked.

"Since I'm breathing, yes." She waved him at the table. "Go sit down. I'll bring you some along with a couple cookie bars."

He gave her a wink. "I should come home early more often." Glancing at Lilah as he walked to the table, he asked, "So you've met my brother. What do you think?"

Micah's gaze snapped to hers and she read worry there. She smiled at him. "I think he was very brave to ride a bus all the way from Arizona by himself."

"Yeah. Brave." Reed sat down, reached out and gave Micah's arm a slight punch. "Also stupid. You were lucky you got here all right."

Micah frowned. "I'm not stupid or anything."

"No, not stupid," Reed agreed, "but walking out and making the school panic enough to call Father wasn't the brightest move."

"Yeah, I know. He already called." Micah looked at Lilah. "She told him to calm down and then she hung up on him."

Lilah actually felt herself flush as Reed turned an interested gaze on her. "Is that right?"

"He was shouting at Micah and I couldn't stand it," she said, throwing her hands up. "Shoot me."

"Hell, no," he said, smiling, "I only wish I'd been here to see it."

Lilah grinned at him. So far so good.

"It was awesome," Micah admitted.

When Connie brought the coffee and cookies, Reed turned his gaze back to his brother. Lilah felt Micah's nerves and knew he was as anxious as she was.

"I don't want to go back," the boy said, his voice hardly more than a whisper. "I hate it there, Reed. They make you wear this dumb uniform and somebody's always telling you what to do and the food sucks, it's all healthy and you can't even eat when you want to—"

He said that last as if he were being force-fed twigs and grass.

"And Mom said I have to stay there this summer, too, and there's only me and two other kids in the whole place over the summer and it's really creepy at night when it's so empty and—"

"Take a breath," Reed advised softly and pushed the cookies toward the boy.

Tears stung the backs of Lilah's eyes. Sunlight glanced in through the windows and lay across the kitchen table in a puddle of gold. Rosie smacked her hands on the food tray, and Connie came up to stand beside Lilah, as if they were building a wall to defend one lonely little boy. The question was, would they need it?

"You can stay here," Reed said, and Micah's gaze lifted to his, hope shining as brightly as the sun.

"Really?" One word, said in a hushed awe that held so much yearning Lilah's heart broke with it.

"Yeah, I hated boarding school, too," Reed said, shaking his head. "It is creepy at night, especially when most of the other kids are gone. We've got plenty of room, so you can spend the summer here and we'll figure out what to do about school in September."

"Really? I can stay?" Micah's voice broke and he wiped his eyes with the backs of his hands.

Lilah released a breath she hadn't even realized she'd been holding. She should have known Reed would come through. Hadn't she seen enough evidence over the past couple of weeks that he wasn't nearly as detached as he pretended to be?

Reed ruffled the boy's hair, then took a sip of his coffee. "I'll clear it with Father and your mother. On one condition…"

Wary now, the boy asked, "What?"

"You have to get rid of that ugly uniform and start wearing jeans and sneakers."

Micah's bottom lip trembled, his eyes went shiny and in a rush of gratitude, he jumped out of his chair and hugged his brother. Lilah's heart swelled as she watched

Reed hug him back, and she shared a smile with Connie. Then Reed caught her gaze over Micah's head and she could have sworn she saw another piece of his personal wall break apart and shatter.

God, she was falling in love. Reed Hudson wasn't a cold man, she thought, he had just been protecting himself for so long, it had become a way of life. His gaze bored into hers and even at a distance, she felt the heated stare right down to her bones.

Yep, she thought. *Love.* There was no future in it. There would be no happy ending. Oh, she was in serious trouble—and the only way out was pain.

A few hours later, Reed reasoned with his father. "Micah can stay with me. He hates that stupid school so why keep him there if I'm offering an alternative?"

A part of him wondered *why* he was offering, but the more sensible part knew exactly why. He had been in Micah's shoes and the memories were still clear enough that he understood just how the kid felt. Sent off to boarding school, allowed home only at Christmas and sometimes during the summer. Otherwise, ignored and endured until school started up again. There was no reason for Micah to go through it any longer.

Besides, the memory of the kid's tears had been burned into Reed's mind and heart and damned if he'd send his brother back to a place that made him miserable.

"We'll spend the summer together and if he's happy, he can go to school here," Reed continued firmly, using the only tone of voice his father respected. "There's a good school just a few blocks from here." He'd made a point to check out the schooling situation *before* confronting his father.

"Even if I'm willing to let him stay, Micah's mother will never agree," Robert Hudson muttered.

"Come on, Father," Reed said with a laugh. "You know Suzanna will be fine with anything that keeps Micah out of her hair."

His father huffed out a breath. "True. I don't know what I was thinking when I married her."

Neither did Reed, but that wasn't the point. Although he would admit that his father had wised up fast. He'd been married to Suzanna only a little more than a year. Then, the money-grubbing woman had disappeared from their lives. Thank God. "So you're okay with Micah staying with me?"

"It's fine," his father said after a long minute. "I'll call the school tomorrow, tell them he won't be back. Then I'll let Micah know."

"Good." Relief that he hadn't had to make a bigger fight of it filled Reed. He'd been willing to go to battle for his younger brother, but the fact that he hadn't had to made everything much easier. "How's Nicole doing? Baby news yet?"

His father sighed. "She's fine, but the doctor says it could be another two weeks."

Hard to believe his father was still out creating children he never seemed to have time for. But Robert kept marrying much younger women who always insisted on having a family of their own.

"Tell her I said hello."

"I will." His father's voice softened. "Thank you. I appreciate it. And on another subject," he continued a moment later, "who told that woman she could hang up on me?"

Reed laughed. "Nobody tells Lilah what to do. She

came up with that solution on her own when you were ranting."

"Huh. Well, I liked her. She's got spine."

Amused, Reed thought that his father had no idea. After he hung up, he sat back in his desk chair and glanced to the corner of his desk. Just last night he and Lilah had been right there, wrapped up in each other, tearing at each other's clothes, mindless to anything but what they were feeling. Instantly his body went hard as stone as memories flooded his brain. He groaned, shifted in his chair and steered his brain away from thoughts of Lilah to focus on his new set of problems.

Last month, he was living in a hotel and had nothing to worry about but his clients and the occasional call for help from a sibling. Now he had a house, a housekeeper, a baby and a twelve-year-old to think about. There was just no way Connie would be able to take care of the house *and* two kids. He was going to need a nanny. And until he found one, he'd need Lilah to stay on.

Though his body liked that idea, his brain was sending out warning signals. But it wasn't as if he had a choice here. He had to work and there were two kids who needed looking after. Surely she'd see that and understand why she had to stay longer than she might have planned.

With that thought firmly in mind, he left his study, headed down the hall to Lilah's room and quietly knocked at the door. The hall was dark but for the night-lights. Rosie's bedroom door was cracked open, but Micah's room was closed up tight. The house was quiet, almost as if it was holding its breath. Just like him.

She opened the door and the first thing he noticed was the scent of strawberries. Her hair was still damp from a shower and lay in waves atop her shoulders. She wore no makeup at all and she was still more beautiful than any woman he'd ever known.

His heart jolted in his chest as his gaze met hers. She wore a bright yellow nightgown, the hem stopping midthigh. It had a scooped neck, short sleeves and was covered in pictures of puppies. All different kinds of puppies, from poodles to German shepherds. For a second or two he couldn't even speak. Finally, though, he lifted his gaze to hers and asked, "Like dogs?"

"What? Oh." She glanced down at herself, then shrugged. "Yeah, I do." Then she frowned. "Is something wrong? The kids okay?"

"Everything's fine," he said quickly, easing the worry that had leaped to life in her eyes. He probably should have waited to speak to her until morning. But it was too late to back out now. "We have to talk, Lilah."

A sinking sensation opened up in the pit of her stomach as soon as she heard those words. Never a good way to start a conversation, she thought, stepping back and waving Reed into her room. Lilah had one instant to wish he hadn't seen her in her puppy nightgown, then that thought fled in favor of other, darker thoughts. She'd known this talk was coming.

Ever since the night before when they'd shared some truly spectacular sex, Lilah had been waiting for Reed to take one giant step backward. But it was all right because she'd already decided that the only way for her to deal with her new feelings for Reed was to leave. As quickly as possible.

She'd seen him in action now, not only with Rose but with Micah, and she could believe that though he maintained safe distances from most people, he wouldn't be cold to children. His gentleness with Micah coupled with his willingness to let the boy move in with him had been the cherry on top of her decision. No one that understanding and kind would be anything less to the baby who'd been left in his care.

Reed paced the confines of the guest room as if looking for something. He raked one hand through his hair and then turned to look at her. "We never talked. About last night, I mean."

"I know. But really," she said, "there's not much to say, is there?" Now that she knew she loved him, Lilah really didn't want to listen to him tell her how there could be nothing between them. How it had just been sex—no matter how life altering. That he wasn't interested in a relationship.

Why not just set the tone right from the beginning? She would be the one to say that she didn't want anything from him. That she had no expectations. Just because her heart would break when she left him didn't mean he had to *know* that.

"Seriously?" He looked surprised, both eyebrows winging up. Then he laughed shortly and shook his head. "Of course you would be different from every other woman I've ever met."

"What's that supposed to mean?" It had sounded like an insult, but he looked almost pleased as he said it.

"It means—" he paused, pulled the curtains at the window back and let the moonlight flood the room "—that every woman I've ever spent the night with woke up with diamonds and wedding bells on her mind."

Lilah laughed a little at that. Well, good. She was happy to be the one different woman in his life. At least, she thought, he'd remember her. If her private dreams were more romantic than she was letting on, they weren't something she was going to share, anyway. Lilah had known going in that there was no future for her and Reed so why pretend otherwise? Why give him the slightest indication that she was disappointed? That she'd miss him? No, thank you. She'd keep her own pain private.

"You're completely safe," she said. "I promise. It was an amazing night, Reed, and I'll never forget it, but it was one night."

Frowning, he said, "Right. I just—never mind. Doesn't matter. So, if we're both clear on last night, there's something else I need to talk to you about."

Lilah sat on the edge of the bed, pulled the hem of her nightgown as far down as she was able and said, "Go ahead."

"The thing is," he said, "I'm going to need you to stay a while longer."

"Oh." She hadn't expected that. Especially after last night, she'd half thought he'd hand her a plane ticket this morning and wave bon voyage from the porch. Which was, she could admit privately, why she had gotten up early and taken Rosie for a walk. She hadn't wanted to hear him explain why he didn't want her.

He walked closer until he stopped right in front of her. Lilah had to tip her head back to meet his eyes. In the moonlight, with his face half in shadow, he looked dangerous, mysterious and so very good. She took a breath and tried to rein in what was no doubt a spill of hormones rushing through her bloodstream. But it wasn't easy, especially since now she knew what it was like to be with him. To have his hands on her, his mouth. She shivered and took another breath.

He scraped one hand across the back of his neck and said, "The thing is, now that Micah's going to be staying here, I can't expect Connie to watch over both kids and take care of this place all by herself."

"True." Lilah's mind started spinning. She really hadn't stopped to think about the logistics of everything. But he was right.

"I'm glad you agree. So look, I need you to stay—"

Her foolish heart leaped.

"—until I can find a nanny."

And then it crashed to the ground.

Oh, God, for her own sake, Lilah knew she should leave. Not only had she left her business alone long enough, but if she stayed on here with Reed, her heart would only get more and more involved. And that would only make eventually leaving that much harder.

"So?" he demanded impatiently.

Lilah smiled. "You really need to work on your patience chakra."

"What?"

"Nothing." Why was it, she wondered, that the man could look so completely irresistible when he was standing there staring at her as if she were speaking Martian? Everything about him appealed to her. From his gruff exterior to the tender lover, to the kind and understanding man he was to his siblings. Lilah was toast and she knew it.

She sighed and stood up, but kept a good foot of space between them. She wouldn't leave him in the lurch. No matter that it might end up costing her, she had to at least help him find the right nanny—for the kids' sakes if nothing else. "Okay, I'll stay."

He blew out a breath and grinned, never knowing

what the power of that smile could do to her. "That's great. Okay."

"But…"

"Always a *but*," he muttered, giving her a wary look. "What is it?"

"I've already been away from my business for two weeks." Lilah had been spending two or three hours every day, checking online and then getting her employees to go into the store to fulfill orders. Her emergency system was working fine, but she'd feel better if she at least checked in, in person. "I need to fly home for the weekend, check on stock and have a meeting with my employees."

He frowned thoughtfully, then said, "All right. How about this? We'll all go."

"What?" Laughing now, she looked up at him in surprise.

"I'm serious." He shrugged. "Micah, Rosie and I will go with you. We can take the family jet this weekend— it'll be more comfortable."

Undeniable, she thought, since she hadn't been looking forward to the flight home even if it was only an hour and a half.

"You can show us the mountains," he was saying, "see your place. Then we'll all come back together."

"You don't have to do that," she said, though she loved the idea of him coming to her town, seeing where she lived. Maybe it would be a way for her to remember him with her once this time with him was over. God, she really was a sap. Having memories of him in her tiny hometown would only make living there without him that much harder. And yet…

"I'd actually like to see the shop where you make all

of the amazing scents that are always clinging to your skin," he murmured, and lifted one hand to sweep her hair back from her face.

She shivered at his touch and held her breath, hoping he'd do more.

"Strawberries tonight." He moved in closer, bent his head to her neck and inhaled, drawing her scent inside him. When he looked into her eyes again, he said, "I like strawberries even more than vanilla."

Her stomach did a slow slide into happy land and her heartbeat jumped into a racing, thundering crash in her chest. Whatever her brain might be worrying over, her body had a whole different set of priorities.

"Do you really think this is a good idea?" she whispered when his mouth was just a breath from hers.

"Probably not," Reed answered. "Do you care?"

"No," she admitted and let him pull her down onto the bed.

His kiss was long and deep and demanding. His hands swept down to snatch up the hem of her nightgown and she trembled as he cupped her breast and rubbed her hardened, sensitive nipple. His tongue dipped into her mouth, tangling with hers in an erotic simulation of just what he wanted to do with her next.

And foolish or not, Lilah was all for it. If she had to give him up, then she might as well enjoy him while she had him, right?

She wrapped her arms around his neck and held on when he rolled them over until she was sprawled on top of him. Then she broke their kiss and looked down into misty green eyes that she would see in her sleep for the rest of her life.

"You're amazing," he whispered, stroking his finger-tips along her cheek, tucking her hair behind her ear.

Her heart felt as if a giant fist were squeezing it tightly and the ache was almost sweet. These few moments with him were all she would have. She wanted to remember everything. Every touch. Every sigh. Every breathless word.

When he bent to kiss her again, Lilah moved to meet him, parting her lips, loving the slide of his tongue against hers. The soft sigh of his breath mingling with her own.

Moonlight flooded the room, silence filled the air and—a long, plaintive wail erupted from the baby moni-tor on the bedside table. Lilah broke the kiss and leaned her forehead against his. Rosie's cry continued to peal into the quiet and Lilah smiled sadly. It was like a sign from the universe.

"I think someone somewhere is trying to tell us some-thing." She gave him a sad smile and rolled off him to stand beside the bed. "I have to go to the baby and you should probably just…go."

"Yeah." He sat up with a resigned half smile on his face. "I'm going to head to bed myself."

They left the room together, each of them going in different directions. A metaphor for their lives, she thought. And even though she would still be with him for a while longer, she knew that tonight signaled an end.

At the threshold of Rosie's room, Lilah paused and murmured, "Goodbye, Reed."

# Nine

Reed hated LA.

But there was no help for it. At least once every couple of weeks, he had to bite the bullet and make the trek into the city.

Today, he had a lunch appointment with a federal judge he'd gone to law school with, followed by a meeting with a prospective new client. Which almost took the sting out of the drive in California's miserable traffic.

Of course the constant stop-and-go on the freeway gave him plenty of time to think, too. Mostly what he was thinking about was that interrupted night with Lilah. He loved Rose, but the baby had lousy timing.

He loved that tiny girl.

Funny, he hadn't really considered that before. He'd spent so much of his life avoiding the mere mention of the word *love*, the fact that it had just popped into his head surprised the hell out of him. But it shouldn't, his ever-logical brain argued. He wasn't a robot, after all. Reed loved his brothers and sisters—it was just the so-called *Love* with a capital *L* he had no interest in.

And wasn't he lucky that Lilah was such a sensible woman? He smiled and nodded to himself, remembering their talk and how well it had gone. Reed couldn't remember a time when he and a woman had been so in sync. So why did he have an itch between his shoulder blades? His satisfied smile faded and became a thoughtful scowl. She could have been a little more reluctant to let go of what they had. Hell, *he* was reluctant.

He'd never in his life been dismissed so completely by a woman. Especially one he still wanted. Reed was usually the one to call a halt. To back off and remind whatever woman he was with that he didn't do forever. That chat never went over well. Until Lilah, he silently admitted. She didn't seem to have a problem walking away and he should be happy about that. Why wasn't he happy about that?

"Even when we're not together she's driving me crazy," he muttered and cursed under his breath when a Corvette cut him off. Still talking to himself, he said, "Now, she's so focused on the kids it's as if she's forgotten I'm even in the house."

For the past few days, he'd hardly seen Lilah. Micah was settling in, making friends in the neighborhood, playing with Rosie and apparently adopting Lilah. The three of them were cozy as hell, with Connie rounding out their happy little group and Reed being drawn in whether he liked it or not.

The hell of it was, he *did* like it. He'd never imagined himself in this situation—a house and kids—but surprisingly enough, it worked for him. The hotel suite had been impersonal, convenient. The house was loud and messy and full of life. There were no empty corners or quiet shadows there and it struck him suddenly how much of his life had been spent in lonely silence. It was only after it had ended that he could actually see *how* he'd been living. Not that it hadn't worked for him. Could still work, he reasoned. It was just that now he knew he liked a different kind of life, too.

What really surprised him about all of this was just how much Reed hated the idea of Lilah leaving. It wasn't about him wanting her there, of course. It was more for the sake of the kids that he worried about it. Though he had to admit that now, every time he thought about the house, he heard Lilah's voice, her laugh, he imagined one of her amazing scents trailing through the air.

Somehow his life had been yanked out of his control.

When his cell phone rang, Reed answered gratefully. Anything to get his mind off Lilah. A moment later, he realized the truth of the old statement "be careful what you wish for."

"Hey, Reed I need a little help."

He rolled his eyes. His half brother on his mother's side hadn't called in a few months. Reed should have known he was due. "Cullen. What's going on?"

A deep, cheerful voice sounded out. "I just need the name of a good lawyer in London."

"What did you do?" Reed's hands fisted on the steering wheel even as his gaze narrowed in concentration on the traffic around him.

"It wasn't me," Cullen said, innocence ringing out proudly in his tone. "It was my car, but I wasn't driving it."

Reed counted to ten, hoping for patience and thought maybe Lilah had had a point about working on his chakras, whatever they were. "What. Happened?"

"A friend was driving the Ferrari and took a bad turn is all."

"A *friend*?"

"Yeah. You'd like her. She's great. Not much of a driver, though."

"Anyone hurt?" Reed clenched his teeth and held his breath. Cullen was the most irresponsible of the whole Hudson/everyone-else bunch. And, he had the habit of going through a long song and dance before finally reaching the bottom line. Cullen was twenty-six and destined to follow his father, Gregory Simmons, into the banking world. God. Reed shuddered to think of Cullen in charge of anyone's money.

"No injuries, the only casualty was a bush."

"What?" He frowned and shook his head, sure he hadn't heard that correctly.

"Juliet mowed down a hundred-year-old shrub and a patch of dahlias." Laughing now, Cullen said, "To hear the woman who lived there going on, you would have thought we'd murdered her beloved dog, not a bloody bush."

"Damn it, Cullen—" Reed's head ached. Sometimes it was a bitch being the oldest.

"Hey, no speeches," his brother interrupted, "just the lawyer, okay?"

Grateful that he wouldn't have to deal with Cullen and the remarkable Juliet, Reed ran through a mental file, then finally said, "Tristan Marks. Call Karen at my office she can give you his number."

And he hoped Tristan would forgive him for this.

"Great, thanks. Knew I could count on you. If I need anything else, I'll call you at home tomorrow, all right?"

"No," Reed said tightly, "it's not all right. I'm going away for the weekend."

Cullen snorted. "Another fascinating law conference?"

"No," Reed said, even more pleased now that he wouldn't be home to deal with anything else Cullen came up with. "I'm taking a couple days off."

There was a pause that lasted long enough that Reed thought for a moment the connection had been lost. Then his brother spoke up again.

"I'm sorry. I think I must have had a small stroke. You said you're taking two days *off*?"

Reed put his blinker on, then changed lanes, preparing to exit. "What's so hard to understand about that?"

"Oh, nothing at all. Miracles happen all the time."

"You're not as amusing as you think you are, Cullen."

"Sure I am," his brother said with a laugh. "So tell me, who is she?"

"She who?"

"The incredible woman with the power to get Reed Hudson away from his desk."

"Go away, Cullen. Call Karen." He hung up with the sound of his brother's laughter ringing in his ears.

Incredible? Yeah, he thought, Lilah really was all of that and more. Just what the hell were they going to do without her?

Utah was prettier than Reed thought it would be. There were a lot of trees, a lot of open space on either side of the freeway and most amazing of all, hardly any

traffic. He actually enjoyed the drive from the airport
to the mountain town of Pine Lake.

The flight was short and he'd had a rental car waiting
for them, complete with car seat for Rosie. It amazed
Reed just how much *gear* was necessary when traveling with kids, though. Good thing they'd taken a private
jet. They would have been waiting for hours at baggage
claim otherwise.

"So do you ski and stuff?" Micah asked from the
backseat.

"I do," Lilah said, half turning in her seat to look at
him. "You'll have to come back in the winter and I'll
take you up the mountain myself."

"Cool!" The kid's face lit up. "Can we, Reed?"

He glanced in the rearview mirror at the eager smile
on his brother's face. "Maybe."

How could he say yes? Lilah was talking about the
winter and Reed knew she wouldn't be a part of their
lives then. If that thought left a gaping hole in his chest,
he didn't have to acknowledge it.

"Turn left here," Lilah said. "We can stop at my house
first, unload everything, then go to the shop."

Reed glanced at her and realized she looked as excited
as Micah. Clearly, she'd missed this place, her home, her
*life*. She'd already given him more than three weeks.
How much more could he ask of her? Hell, he was going
to owe her forever, and he didn't like the sound of that.

Following her directions, he finally turned into the
driveway of what looked like an oversize box. As first
impressions went, he could only think how small it was.
The house was a perfect square, with black shutters
against white siding and a porch that ran the length of
the house. The yard was wide and deep, with the house

sitting far back from the road. There were at least a dozen trees shading the property and Reed thought that somehow the house fit Lilah.

She jumped out of the car, grabbed Rosie and headed for the house, with Micah close on her heels. Reed followed more slowly, watching her, enjoying the view of her backside in black jeans. Once inside, he saw the place was as small as it had appeared, but it also had a cozy feel to it. There were warm colors, soft fabrics and plenty of windows to let in the light.

"Micah, you and Rosie will share a room tonight, okay?"

"Sure." The boy shrugged and picked up his backpack. "Where?"

"Top of the stairs on the right."

Reed watched him go, silently marveling at the change in his little brother. Just a few days away from the boarding school and the boy had relaxed and smiled more than Reed ever remembered him doing.

When he was alone with Lilah, Reed said, "I like your house."

"Thanks," she said, turning a grin up to him. "I know it's tiny, but it's all I've ever needed. I've got the kitchen and the mudroom set up as my workshop and that's worked pretty well up until now. But I may have to add on at some point."

Nodding, he couldn't help thinking that there was plenty of room at his house to build a huge workshop for her where she could make all the soaps and stuff she wanted. But, his brain reminded him, she wouldn't be there to use it, would she?

Scowling now, he paid attention when she went on.

"The house is still a work in progress and it's only

got two bedrooms, so Micah and Rosie aren't the only ones who'll have to share a room..."

One eyebrow arched. Things were looking up. "Really? Well, now I like your house even more."

Wryly, she said, "I thought you might feel that way."

After they got settled in, they all walked to the center of town and Reed had to admit there was something about the place that appealed. He'd never thought of himself as a small-town kind of guy, but walking down the main street, with its bright flowers tumbling out of half barrels, old-fashioned streetlights and buildings that looked at least a hundred years old, he could see the charm of it. And when they got a tour of Lilah's shop Reed was definitely impressed.

The shop was bright and clean and so tidy, there wasn't a thing out of place. Shelves were lined with the famous soaps in a rainbow of colors, many of them wrapped together by ribbon to be sold as sets. There were candles as well, and tiny bottles filled with lotions in the same scents as the soaps.

Lilah had built something good here, Reed thought, and he felt a stir of admiration for her. When her employees hurried in for a spontaneous meeting, he watched Lilah's happiness as she listened to all the latest news and he realized just how much she'd given up to stay with him and help with Rosie. These were Spring's friends, the town his sister had called home, and Reed listened to stories about her that made him smile and wish again that he and Spring hadn't been at odds when she died.

The rest of the afternoon passed quickly, with exploring the town, stopping for dinner and then walking to a lake so Micah could throw bread to overfed ducks. It was the first time in years that Reed had actually slowed down long enough to enjoy the moment. And being there, walking through a soft night with Lilah and the kids, brought him a kind of peace he'd never known before.

That worried him. He was getting far too used to Lilah. And that was a bad move. She wasn't staying with him. There was no future waiting for them. There was only now.

"Are you okay?" Lilah's voice came softly, since the kids were asleep in the room across the hall.

"Yeah, why?"

"I don't know, you seem…distracted."

"It's nothing. Just thinking about work."

She laughed and climbed into bed. "Let it go, Reed. You're allowed to *not* work once in a while, you know?"

"You're right," he said, looking down at her. "You want to guess what I'm thinking about now?"

She smiled, a slow, deliberate curve of her mouth that sent jolts of lightning spearing through him. "That's too easy."

He joined her in the bed and pulled her in close, holding her body pressed along his length as he dipped his head to kiss her. That first taste spiraled through him and the jagged edges inside him softened. This moment was everything, he realized. Thoughts, worries, problems could all wait. For now, all he wanted was her.

She moved into him and he slid one hand down her body to explore her heat, her curves, the luscious lines of her. She was so responsive, it pushed him higher and faster than he'd ever been before. She scraped her hands up and down his back and he felt every touch like tiny brands, scoring into his skin.

They moved together in silence, hushed breath, whispered words, quiet movements. When he entered her body, there was almost a sigh of sound and the rhythm he set was slow, tender. He looked down at her and lost himself in her eyes. She touched his face, drew him down for a kiss and he swallowed her moan of pleasure as she reached the peak they were each racing toward. A moment later, he joined her, bending his head to hers, taking the scent of her with him as he fell.

In the quiet aftermath, lying in the dark, entwined to-gether, Reed heard Rosie stirring. A few minutes more, he knew she'd be howling, waking Micah up, as well.

"I'll be right back," he whispered and walked naked from the room. When he came back, he was carrying the sniffling baby, who lit up like Christmas when she saw Lilah.

Reed lay down in the bed and set Rosie down be-tween them.

The baby cooed and clapped and giggled, happy now because she wasn't alone in the dark.

"When she falls asleep, I'll put her back in her bed," Reed said, dropping a kiss on the baby's forehead.

"That might take a while," Lilah answered, while Rosie played with her fingers.

"We've got time." Not much, he told himself, but they had right now.

As he lay there, watching the woman and child com-municating in smiles and kisses, Reed realized that it felt as if they were a family. And he scowled into the darkness.

"I have some bad news," Reed said, dropping his briefcase onto the nearest chair. He gave a quick glance around at the Malibu beach house Carson Duke had been living in since splitting with his wife. The place was bright, lots of white and blue, and it sat practically on the sand. With the French doors open, he could hear the rush and roar of the sea.

Carson turned to look at Reed, worry sparking in his eyes. "Tia? Is she okay?"

Amazing, Reed thought. Even though they were in the middle of a divorce, the man reacted as if they were still lovers, still committed to each other. Fear came off Carson Duke in thick, fat waves until Reed assured him, "She's fine. But she wouldn't sign off on the property issues, so we'll be going to mediation in a judge's chambers."

Carson actually slumped in relief, then gave a shaky laugh and scraped one hand across his face. "Thank God. The mediation doesn't matter. As long as she's okay." He turned, walked through the open doors onto the stone terrace and tipped his face into the wind. Reed walked outside to join him and took a moment to look around.

Despite the gloomy weather, there were dozens of surfers sitting on their boards, waiting for the next wave. And laid out like elegant desserts on a table, women in barely there bikinis draped themselves on towels in artful poses.

Reed stared out at the slate gray water. "If you don't mind me saying so, you just don't sound like my regular about-to-be-ex-husband divorce client."

One half of Carson's mouth quirked into a humorless smile. "Guess not. I told you before, I never expected Tia and me to end up like this." He frowned at the ocean. "I can't even tell you where things went to hell, either." Glancing at Reed, he asked, "I should know, shouldn't I? I mean, I should know *why* we're getting this divorce, right?"

Normally, Reed would have given Carson the usual spiel about how he was getting a divorce because he and his wife had agreed it wasn't working. But somehow that sounded lame and generic to him now. Oddly enough, Reed and Carson had sort of become friends through this process and he felt he owed the man more than platitudes.

"I don't know, Carson." Reed tucked his hands into his pockets. "Sometimes I think things just go wrong and it's impossible to put your finger on exactly when it happened."

Carson snorted. "Thought you said you'd never been through this. You talk like a survivor."

"I am, in a way," he said thoughtfully. "My parents love being married. Repeatedly. Between them I have ten siblings with another due anytime now."

Carson whistled, low and long, whether in admiration or sympathy, Reed couldn't be sure.

"I had a front-row seat for way too many divorces as a kid and I can tell you that neither of my parents would be able to say *why* they got those divorces." To this day Reed had no idea why his parents jumped from marriage to marriage, always looking for perfect, never satisfied. Sadly, he didn't think they knew why, either. He only knew that they'd made themselves and their children miserable. If that was what love looked like, you could keep it.

"You're in this now, Carson," he said quietly. "And even if you can't recall the reason for it, there *was* one. You and Tia both want to end it, so maybe it's better if you just accept what is and move on."

The other man thought about that for a long minute or two, then muttered, "Yeah, logically I know you're right. But I know something else, too. Acceptance is a bitch."

"Thanks for coming, really. I'll call the agency when the decision's been made." Lilah smiled and waved the third nanny candidate on her way, then closed the door and leaned back against it.

Honestly, these interviews were awful. She hated talking to a steady stream of women all vying for the opportunity to take care of the kids *Lilah* loved. How was she supposed to choose? Young and energetic? Older and more patient? There was no perfect nanny and there was absolutely *no* way to guarantee that the women would even like Micah and Rosie. Or that the kids would like them.

Pushing away from the door, Lilah threw a glance at the kitchen, where Connie was giving Rose her lunch. Lilah should probably go back there, but she wanted a few minutes to herself first.

Plopping down into an overstuffed chair in the living room, she pulled her cell phone out of her pocket and scrolled to the photo gallery. Flipping past image after image, taken last weekend in Utah, she smiled. Micah feeding the ducks. Rosie trying to eat a pinecone. Micah and Reed riding a roller coaster at the Lagoon amusement park. Rosie trying her first ice-cream cone, then "sharing" it with Reed by smacking him in the face with it.

Lastly, Lilah stared down at the image of all four of them. She had asked a stranger to take the picture, wanting at least one with them all grouped together. They were all smiling. Lilah's arm hooked through Reed's, Micah holding Rose and leaning into Reed. "A unit." That's what she felt when she looked at the picture.

For the length of that weekend, it had felt as if they were a family, and for a little while, Lilah had indulged herself by pretending. But really, they weren't a family at all.

Her heart hurt. That was the sad truth. Lilah looked at these pictures, then imagined leaving them all and a sharp, insistent pain sliced at her. How was she supposed to walk away? She loved those kids. But more, she loved *Reed*. The problem was, she knew he wouldn't want to hear it.

"Well, maybe he should anyway," she told herself. Wasn't she the one who'd said people change? Reed had already changed a lot as far as she could see. He'd taken Rosie and Micah into his life and was making it work. Why not welcome *love* into his life, too?

She scrolled to a picture of Reed, smiling at her, sunlight dancing in his eyes. Trailing one finger over his face, she whispered, "Even if you don't want it, you should know that I love you."

Sighing, she stood up and tucked her phone back into her pocket before heading to the kitchen. Connie was at the table, feeding Rose, who happily slapped both hands on her tray. Stopping long enough to pour herself some coffee from the always-ready pot, Lilah then took a seat opposite Connie.

"So," the older woman asked, "how was contestant number three?"

Lilah sighed and cupped her coffee between her palms. "She was fine, I guess. Seemed nice enough, even if she did keep checking her phone to see if there was something more interesting going on somewhere else."

Connie clucked her tongue and shook her head. "Cell phones are the death of civilization."

Smiling, Lilah said, "She's young—so she'll either learn to not text during interviews or she won't find a job." Taking a sip of coffee, she glanced out the window at the backyard. "Where's Micah?"

"Down the street playing basketball with Carter and Cade."

"Good." She nodded. "He needs friends."

"And what do you need?" Connie asked.

Lilah looked back to her. "World peace?"

"Funny, and nice job of dodging the question."

"I don't know what to do," Lilah said. "I haven't found the right nanny, I can't stay here indefinitely and—" Since they'd been back in California, Reed had spent so much time at work she hardly saw him. A reaction to the closeness they'd shared in Utah? Was he silently letting her know that the family vibe she'd felt in Utah wasn't something he wanted? Was he trying to convince her to leave without actually saying it?

"I know," Connie said softly. "It's the *and* that's the hardest to live with."

Reacting to the sympathy in Connie's voice, she said, "Yeah, it is."

"Well, I can't do anything about that." Connie took a baby wipe, cleaned up Rosie's hands, then, while the tiny girl twisted her head trying to avoid it, wiped her mouth, too. Lifting the tray off, she scooped Rosie up, plopped her down on her lap, then looked at Lilah. "I do have something to say on the nanny front, though."

"What is it?"

"I'm a little insulted, is what." Connie waved a hand when Lilah started to protest that she'd never intended to insult her. "You haven't done a thing, honey. If Reed Hudson thinks I can't ride herd on one twelve-year-old, look after a baby who's as good as gold and take care of a house, well, he's out of his mind." Connie jiggled Rosie until the little girl's giggles erupted like bubbles.

Smiling, the woman continued, "Am I so old I can't watch over two kids? I don't think so. We don't need a nanny. What these kids need is a mom. And until they get that, they have a Connie."

*Mom.*

Lilah's heart squeezed again. Like the prospective nanny she'd just said goodbye to, she'd been interviewing for the job she wanted but would never have. She wasn't Mom. She wasn't going to be. Unless she took a chance and told Reed how she felt. At this point, she asked herself, what did she have to lose?

"Good point, Connie," Lilah said, with another sip of coffee. "I know Reed was trying to make your life easier..."

"When I need that, I'll say so."

Lilah chuckled. "I'll tell Reed you said so."

"Oh, don't you bother," the other woman assured her. "I'll tell him myself, first thing. I've been biting my tongue and it's past time Reed got an earful."

It was, Lilah thought, past time that Reed heard a lot of things.

Later that evening, Reed was shut up in his study, going over a few of the details for several upcoming cases. Focus used to come easily. Now he had to force himself to concentrate on paperwork that had once fascinated him. Organization had always been the one constant in his life. Even as a kid, he'd been the one to know where everyone was, where they were going and what they were doing once they got there. Now his life was up in the air and his brain was constantly in a fog.

At the knock on his door, Reed gave up trying to work and called, "Come in."

Lilah stepped into the room, smiled then slowly walked toward him. She was wearing white shorts, a red T-shirt and sandals and somehow managed to look like the most beautiful thing he'd ever seen. Hell, he could watch her move forever, he thought. She had an innate grace that made her steps seem almost like a ballet. Her hair caught the lamplight in the room and seemed to sizzle with an inner fire. Her eyes, though, were what caught and held him. There were secrets there and enough magic to keep a man entranced for a lifetime.

*A lifetime?*

Reed took a breath and told himself to ease back. This wasn't forever. This was *now* and there was nothing wrong with living in the moment. He'd been doing it his whole damn life and he was doing fine, wasn't he?

"Am I interrupting?" she asked.

He glanced down at the files on his desk and the one open on his computer monitor, then shrugged. "Not really. Can't seem to concentrate right now, anyway. What's up?"

"I have something for you." She held out a picture frame and when he took it, Reed smiled.

"The one the man with the snow cone took of the four of us at the amusement park."

She came around the edge of the desk and looked

down at the photo with him. "Yeah. I printed it out and framed it for you. I thought maybe you might like it for in here or at the office."

The weekend in Utah seemed like a long time ago, but looking at the picture brought it all back again. Micah laughing and forcing Reed onto every roller coaster at the park. The kid was fearless so how could Reed not be? Even though a couple of them had given him a few gray hairs. And Rosie so happy all the damn time, clapping at the animals at the zoo, eating ice cream for the first time and doing a whole-body shiver at the cold. His mouth quirked into a smile as he remembered that one perfect day.

Then his gaze landed on Lilah's smiling face in the photo and everything in him twisted into a tangle of lust and heat and...more. The four of them looked like a family. At that thought, he shifted uneasily in his chair. "It's great," he said, looking up at her. "Thanks."

"You're welcome." She perched on the edge of his desk and her bare, lightly tanned leg was within stroking distance. He didn't succumb. "Connie wanted to talk to you about—"

He held up one hand. "The nanny thing and yeah, she's already let me know where she stands on the whole situation."

Lilah smiled and her eyes twinkled. "She was pretty insistent that she can handle two kids and a house."

"I have no doubt about it," Reed said with a wince as he remembered the housekeeper giving him what for just an hour ago. "By the time she was finished with me, I felt like I was ten years old and about to be sentenced to washing dishes again."

Her smile widened. "She really loves you."

"I know that, too," he admitted wryly. "I was only trying to make life easier on her but now she's convinced I think of her as some useless old woman, though I think she was making that up to get her way, which she did, obviously."

"So no nanny?"

"No." He couldn't really argue with Connie when she'd hit him with one question in particular. *"Didn't you have enough of nannies in and out of your life when you were a boy? Do you really want to do the same damn thing to those kids?"* And no, he didn't. If Connie wanted to handle everything, then he had no problem with it.

"Well, then," Lilah said quietly, "that brings me to why I'm really here interrupting your work."

Reed swiveled his desk chair around so that he was facing her. Her eyes seemed dark and deep and for some reason, the back of his neck started prickling.

"I was only staying on to help find a nanny," she was saying, "and, since you're not going to hire one…"

She was leaving. She'd come in here, smelling of—he took a breath—green apples, and looking like a summer dream to tell him she was leaving. His stomach fisted, but he held on to his poker face for all the good it would do him.

"You don't have to go," he said before he could talk himself out of it.

She blew out a nervous breath. "Well, that's something else I wanted to talk to you about."

He smiled slowly, hoping she was about to say that she didn't want to leave. That she wanted to stay there with them. With him.

"I love you."

As if a bucket of ice had been dumped in his lap,

Reed went stone still. He didn't have to fake a poker face now, because it felt as if he'd been drained of all emotion. "What?"

Her eyes locked on to his and heat and promise filled them.

"I love you, Reed. And I love the kids." She reached over, picked up the photo and showed it to him again as if he hadn't been staring at it a moment before. "I want us to be the family we look like we already are." She reached out and gently smoothed his hair back from his forehead. Reed instinctively pulled back from her touch.

She flinched, fingers curling into a fist.

Jumping up from the chair he couldn't sit still in a moment longer, Reed took a few quick steps away then whirled back around. "This wasn't part of the plan, Lilah."

She pushed off the desk and stood facing him, chin lifted, eyes shining. Tears? he wondered. "Falling in love with you wasn't in my plan, either, but it happened."

He choked back a sound that was half laugh and half groan. *Be a family.* Instantly, the faces of clients, hundreds of them, flashed through his mind. Each and every one of them had started out in "love." Built families. Counted on the future. None of them had gone into marriage expecting to divorce, but they all had. And that wasn't even counting his own damn family.

"Not gonna happen," he said shortly, shaking his head for emphasis—convincing her? Or himself? "I'll never get married—"

"I wasn't proposing."

"Sure you were," he countered, then waved one hand at her. "Hell, look at you. You've got white picket fence all over you."

"What are you—" Her eyes flashed in the lamplight and it wasn't love shining there now, but a building anger that was much safer—for both of them.

He didn't let her talk. Hell, if he'd known this was what had been cooking in her brain, he'd have cut her off long ago. "Yeah, I like being with you and the sex is amazing. You're great with the kids and they're nuts about you. But that's it, Lilah.

"I've seen too much misery that comes from love and I'm not going to get pulled into the very trap that I spend every day trying to dig other people out of."

He saw hurt tangle with the anger in her eyes and hated being the cause of it. But better for her to know the truth than to hatch dreams that would never come true. It tore at Reed to lose her, though—and then an idea occurred to him. Maybe, just maybe, there was a small chance they could salvage something out of this.

"You could stay," he blurted out and took a step toward her before stopping again. "This isn't about love, Lilah. I won't get married. I won't be in love. But I do like you a hell of a lot. We work well together and the kids need you. Hell, I could pay *you* to be their nanny, then Connie would get the help she needs without being offended."

"You'd pay me…"

He took another step. "Anything you want. And I'll build a workshop onto the back of the house. You could make your soaps and lotions and stuff in there and ship them to your store in Utah. Or hell, open a store here in Laguna. We're a big crafts town. You could be a franchise." Another step. "And best of all, we could be together and risk nothing."

Lilah shook her head and sighed heavily. Sorrow was

etched into her features and the light in her eyes faded as he watched.

"If you risk nothing," she said softly, "you gain nothing. I won't be your bought-and-paid-for lover—"

Shocked, Reed argued, "I didn't say that. Didn't think it."

"Paying me to stay here while we continue to have sex amounts to the same thing," she told him.

"That's insulting," he said tightly. "To both of us."

"Yeah," she said. "I thought so. I'm going home, Reed. I'll leave tomorrow. I want to see the kids and say goodbye, then I'll go."

Though she hadn't moved a step, Reed thought she might as well have been back in Utah already. He couldn't reach her. And maybe that was best. Whatever it was they'd shared was over and was quickly descending into the kind of mess he'd managed to avoid for most of his life.

Turning, she headed for the door and he let her go.

It was the hardest thing he'd ever done.

# Ten

The next month was a misery.

Lilah tried to jump back into her normal life, but there was another life hanging over her head and she couldn't shake it. She missed Rosie and Micah and Connie.

And being without Reed felt as though someone had ripped her heart out of her chest. Every breath was painful. Every memory was both comfort and torture. Every moment without those she loved tore at her.

"Are you sure you did the right thing?"

Lilah sighed and focused on her mother's concerned face on the computer screen. Thank God for video calls, she thought. It helped ease the distance while her mother and Stan were off on their never-ending cruise. Of course, the downside to video chats was her mother could see far more than she would have on the phone.

The ship had just made port in London and since it

was her mother's favorite city, Lilah knew that as soon as she was through with this chat, her mom and Stan would be out shopping and sightseeing. But for now, Lilah was telling her all about Rose and Micah and, most especially, Reed.

"I really didn't have a choice, Mom." Lilah had thought through this situation from every possible angle and there just had been no way for her to stay and keep her pride. Her dignity. Her sense of self.

If she'd given in to her own wants and Reed's urgings, she would have eventually resented him and been furious with herself for settling for less than they both deserved.

"No," her mother said softly, "I suppose you didn't. But I think, from everything you've told me, that the idiot man *does* love you."

Lilah laughed a little and it felt good. It seemed as though she hadn't really smiled or laughed since she left California. Behind her mother, Stan came up from somewhere in their suite, bent over and said, "Hi, sweetie! I'm going to have to go with your mother on this one. He does love you. He's just too scared to admit it."

Frowning now, Lilah said, "Nothing scares Reed."

Stan grinned and she had to smile back. He wasn't exactly the image of a millionaire businessman in his short-sleeved bright green shirt and his bald head shining in the overhead lights. It was impossible to not love Stan. Especially since his one desire was to make her mother happy.

"Honey, real *love* scares every man alive." He kissed the top of her mother's head. "Well, except for me. By the time I met your mom, I'd been alone so long that one look at her and I knew. She was the one I'd been waiting for. Looking for. And when you're alone all your life, you grab hold of love when it comes along and you never let it go."

"Oh," her mother said, turning her head to kiss her husband's cheek. "You are the sweetest man. For that, we can go to the London Imperial War Museum again."

Stan winked at Lilah, then grinned again. "I'll let you two talk, then. Just don't give up on the guy, okay, honey?"

Sighing a little, Lilah promised and then when it was just her mother and her again, she said, "I'm glad you've got Stan."

"Me, too," her mom answered. "Even when the ship docks in London and I'm dragged through that war museum again. But that's something for you to remember, too. Your father was an amazing man and I was lucky to love him for all those years." Smiling, she leaned toward the screen and said, "But, he was scared spitless to get married. He even broke up with me when it looked like we were getting serious."

Surprised, Lilah said, "You never told me that."

"You never needed to hear it before now. *Forever* is a big word and can shake even the strongest man. Your dad came around—but not until he got the chance to miss me."

Lilah thought about that and wondered.

"If you need me all you have to do is say so, honey. I'll catch the first flight out of Heathrow and catch up with Stan and the ship later."

Because her mother absolutely would throw her own life to the winds to support her daughter, Lilah realized again just how lucky she was. In spite of the turmoil in her life right at the moment, she had stability and love. And that was more than Reed had ever had.

"Thanks, Mom. But I'm fine." She straightened in her chair and nodded. "I've got the shop and my friends and…it'll get better."

"It will," her mother promised. "You are the best daughter ever and you deserve to have the kind of love that fairy tales are made of."

Tears stung her eyes but Lilah blinked them back.

"I *know* this will all work out just the way it's supposed to," her mother continued. "And like Stan said, I wouldn't give up hope yet. After some time to think and to really miss you, I'm willing to bet that Reed Hudson is going to realize that life without Lilah just isn't worth living."

Reed had made it through the longest month of his life.

He wasn't sure how, since thoughts of Lilah had haunted him day and night. *I love you.* Those three words had echoed over and over again in his mind. He heard her voice, saw her eyes and felt again his own instinctive withdrawal.

*I love you.*

No one had ever said that to him before. Not once in his whole damn life had Reed ever heard those words. And the first time he did, he threw them back in her face.

"What the hell…" Scraping one hand across his face, Reed pushed everything but work out of his mind. He didn't have any right to be focusing on his own life when someone was *paying* him to focus on his.

"You okay?" Carson Duke asked in a whisper.

"Yeah," Reed assured him, "fine. Look, we'll just get through the mediation and we'll be back on track. The judge will keep everything on track, you and Tia will decide how you want things done and it's over."

Nodding, Carson inhaled sharply, then exhaled the same way. "Gotta say, best thing about this mediation is seeing Tia. It feels like forever since I've been close to her."

Reed knew just how the other man felt. He hadn't seen Lilah in a month and it felt like a year. It hadn't helped that the kids were complaining, missing her as much as he was. Well, Micah was complaining, demanding that they go to Utah and get her, while Rosie just cried, as if she were inconsolable. Then there was Connie, who took every opportunity to sneer at him and mention how lonely the house felt without Lilah's laughter.

He was being punished for doing the right thing.

How did that make sense?

But if letting her go was the right thing, then why did it feel so wrong?

"Tia." Carson shot out of his chair and turned to face the woman walking into the room beside her lawyer, Teresa Albright.

Reed knew Teresa well. She was a hell of an attorney and had always been a good friend. But today, her sleek red hair only reminded him of Lilah's red-gold waves and he found he resented Teresa for even being there.

"Carson," Tia said as she stepped up to the table. The legendary singer had long black hair and big brown eyes. Those eyes as she looked at her husband were warm and her smile was tentative. "How are you?"

"I'm all right," Carson answered. "You?"

Reed watched the byplay and could feel the tension in the room. Hell, Carson looked as if he was ready to launch himself across the table, and the way Tia was wringing her hands together made it seem she was doing everything she could to keep from reaching for him. Reed was relieved when the judge showed up and they were forced to take their seats.

"Everyone here?" the judge asked as he walked into the meeting room at the courthouse and settled into the chair at the head of the table. At the nods he received in answer, the man said, "All right, let's get this show on the road. Why don't we start with the houses and work from there?"

The Hollywood Hills house went to Tia and the lodge in Montana to Carson. No arguments slowed things down and Reed wondered why in the hell they were even there. The two people appeared to be willing to work together, so why hadn't Tia just signed off on everything in the first place?

"Concerning the Malibu house and its contents," Teresa was saying, "my client wants Mr. Duke to retain possession."

"No," Carson blurted out, glancing first at Reed, then to Tia. "You should have that place," he said.

"No, I want you to have it," Tia argued.

Both Teresa and Reed tried to shush their clients—it was rarely productive for the parties involved to get into conversations. Best to leave it to the attorneys. But this time, no one was listening.

"You love that house," Carson said softly.

Tia nodded and bit her bottom lip. "I do, but you do, too. Carson, you built the brick barbecue on the terrace by hand. And you laid the stone terrace."

"*We* laid the stone terrace," Carson reminded her, a half smile on his face. "Remember, we started out in the afternoon and refused to stop until it was finished?"

Tia smiled, too, but her eyes were teary and the sunlight spearing in through the windows made those tears shine like diamonds. "I remember. We wouldn't quit. We just kept going, and we finally laid that last stone at three in the morning."

"We celebrated with champagne," Carson said softly.

"Then we lay on the patio and watched a meteor shower until nearly dawn," she said sadly.

"Damn it, Tia, why are we even here?" Carson stood up and planted both hands on the table, leaning toward his wife. "I don't want this. I want *you*."

"Carson..." Reed warned.

"No." He glanced at Reed, shook his head and looked back at the woman he didn't want to lose. "I love you, Tia."

"What?" She stood up, too, in spite of Teresa's hand at her elbow trying to tug her back into her seat.

"I love you," Carson repeated, louder this time. "Always have. Always will. I don't know how the hell we got to this ugly little room—"

"Hey," the judge complained, "we just had the place redecorated."

"But we don't belong here," Carson said earnestly, ignoring everyone but his wife. "I made a promise to you. To love you and cherish you till the end of my life, and I don't want to break that promise, Tia. Just like when we built that damn terrace, I don't want us to quit."

"Me, either, Carson," she said, smiling through the tears already spilling down her cheeks. "I never wanted this divorce. I'm not sure how this even happened, but I've missed you so much. I love you, Carson. I always will."

"Stay married to me, Tia." He was talking faster now,

as if his life depended on getting his words right, and maybe it did.

"Yes. Oh, yes." Her smile brightened, her eyes sparkled in the overhead light.

"Hell, let's take a couple years off," he said. "We'll go to the lodge in Montana and lose ourselves. Maybe make some babies."

She grinned at him. "That sounds wonderful. I don't want to lose you, Carson."

"Babe, you're never going to lose me." He slid across the table, swept his wife into his arms and pulled her in for a kiss that would have sent their fans into a deep sigh of satisfaction.

Hell, even Reed felt as if he was watching a movie unfold. When the happy couple left the office a few minutes later after abject apologies for wasting their attorneys' time, Reed thought about everything that had happened. He'd never before lost a divorce to marriage and he found himself hoping that Carson and Tia really could make their life together work.

Carson had taken a chance, fought for what he wanted—and he'd won. Hell, Tia and Carson had *both* won.

A *promise*. That's what Carson had called his marriage vows. Giving your word to someone, promising to be faithful. To be there.

As if an actual lightbulb flashed on in his brain, Reed suddenly understood. Marriage wasn't a risk if you trusted the person you were going into it with. Giving your word, keeping it? Well, hell, Reed Hudson had never gone back on his word in his life. And he knew Lilah was the same.

Love wasn't the misery. It was the heart of a promise that could change a life.

Now all he had to do was hope that the woman he wanted would be willing to listen.

Lilah's Bouquet was doing a booming business. Her new shop manager, Eileen Cooper, was working out great and though Lilah still missed Spring, life marched on. Being able to count on Eileen, letting her move into the apartment over the shop, had actually helped Lilah get through—not *over*—Spring's loss.

Plus, burying herself in work had helped Lilah survive a different kind of loss. Her dreams of a happy-ever-after with Reed and the kids were gone and their absence created a dark, empty space inside her that ached almost continuously. So keeping busy also left her little time to wallow.

The past month hadn't been easy, but she'd made it through and every day she got that much closer to maybe someday finding a way to get over Reed. She laughed to herself at the idea. Good luck getting over someone you couldn't stop thinking about, or dreaming about.

She was even thinking of buying a new bed. One that didn't have memories of sex with Reed imprinted into the fabric. Probably wouldn't help, though, because the man was etched into her mind and heart permanently.

"This is wonderful," Sue Carpenter said, shattering Lilah's thoughts, for which she was grateful. The woman hustling up to the counter held a soap and lotion set in one of Lilah's newest scents. "Summer Wind? Beautiful name and I absolutely love the scent. Makes me feel like I'm at the beach!"

"Thanks, Sue," Lilah said, taking the woman's things

and ringing them up. "I really like it, too. Makes me think of summer." And Laguna, and a house on the cliffs where everything she loved lived without her.

"Well, it's wonderful." Sue had no idea that Lilah's thoughts had just spun her into a well of self-pity. "Will you be making candles in that scent, too?"

Lilah forced a smile. Sue was one of her best customers and a great source of publicity for the shop since she told everyone she met all about Lilah's Bouquet. "You bet. I'll have some ready for sale by next week."

"Then I'll be back, but for now, I need a few of the lemon sage candles and might as well get three of the cinnamon, as well." She grinned. "I like to give them to my buyers with the sale of a house."

"That's so nice, thank you." More publicity, since the name of Lilah's store and the address were on the bottom of every candle. Once she had Sue's purchases bagged, she said goodbye and walked over to help another woman choose the right soaps for her.

"I just can't make up my mind," the woman said, letting her gaze sweep around the crowded shop. When she spotted something in particular, though, she murmured softly, "Never mind. I've decided. I'll take one of those. To go."

Smiling, Lilah turned to see what the woman was looking at and actually *felt* her jaw drop. Reed was walking into her store, looking through the crowd, searching for her. When he spotted her, he smiled and a ball of heat dropped into the pit of her stomach. Lilah's mouth went dry and her heartbeat jumped into a fast gallop. What was he doing here? What did it mean?

*Oh, God*, she told herself, *don't read too much into*

*this. Don't pump your hope balloon so high that when it pops you crash back to earth in a broken heap.*

But he was walking toward her, sliding in and out of the dozen or so female customers as if he didn't even see them. Lilah's gaze was locked with his and for the first time since she'd met him, she couldn't tell what he was thinking. That poker face he was so proud of was in full effect. But for the smile, his features were giving nothing away. So by the time he reached her, nerves were alive and skittering through her system.

"God, you look good," he said and the warmth in his voice set off tiny fires in her bloodstream. "Damn it, I missed you."

"I missed you, too," she said softly, not even noticing when the woman she'd been assisting slowly melted away. It was as if there was no one else in the shop. Just the two of them.

August sunshine made the store bright and she told herself that's why her eyes were watering. Because she wouldn't be foolish enough to cry and let Reed know how much it meant to see him again.

"What're you doing here?" she asked, when he only continued to stare down at her and smile.

"I came for you," he said simply.

Somewhere close by, a woman sighed heavily.

"Came for me?" Lilah asked. Did he think she'd go back to California with him just because she'd missed him so much her heart ached every day and night? She couldn't. Wouldn't. Loving him didn't mean that she was willing to set aside who she was for the sake of being with him.

"Reed…" She shook her head and tried to tamp down

the oh-so-familiar ache in the center of her chest. "Nothing's changed. I still can't—"

"I love you," he said, gaze locked with hers.

She swayed unsteadily. He loved her?

"That's a huge change for me, Lilah. I've never said those words before. Never wanted to." His gaze moved over her before coming back to her eyes. "Now I never want to stop."

Lilah gasped and held her breath, half afraid to move and break whatever spell this was that had given her the one thing she had wanted most.

He moved in closer, into her space, looming over her so that she had to tilt her head back to meet his eyes. Laying both hands on her shoulders, he held on tightly as if worried she might make a break for it. Lilah could have told him that even if she wanted to, she didn't think her legs would carry her. As it was, she locked her knees to keep from dissolving into a puddle at his feet.

"I've done a lot of thinking in the last month," he said, scraping his hands up and down her arms to create a kind of friction that seemed to set her soul on fire. "In fact, all I've really done is think about you. And us. And how much I need you. The truth is, the house is empty without you in it."

"Oh, Reed," she said on a soft sigh.

"Noisy as hell and still empty," he said, giving her a half smile that tugged at her heart and made her want to reach up and cup his face in her palms. But she didn't. She needed to hear it all.

"The kids miss you—"

"I miss them, too," she said, the pain she felt staining her words.

"And Connie's so furious with me she keeps burning dinner. On purpose."

Lilah laughed, though it sounded a little watery through the tears clogging her throat. "So they made you come?"

"No," he said, shaking his head and smiling at her as his gaze moved over her face like a caress. "Nobody *makes* me do anything. I came because I don't want to live without you anymore, Lilah. I don't think I can stand it." His eyes burned, his features were tight with banked emotion. "And I finally realized that I don't *have* to live without the woman I want. The woman I love."

"What are you saying?" Lilah's question sounded breathless, anxious.

"That I figured it out," he said, tightening his hold on her. "A couple of days ago, I watched one of my clients back out of a divorce because he was willing to fight for what he wanted. And I realized that the problem isn't that divorce is easy—it's that marriage takes work. It takes two people who want it badly enough to fight for it."

"Reed—"

"Not finished yet," he said, his eyes boring into hers. "No one in my family is a hard worker, which explains the marital failures in the Hudson clan. But I *do* work hard and I never quit when I want something. I'm willing to do whatever it takes to make sure we succeed. The only thing I'm not willing to do is live without you. Not one more day, Lilah."

Her heart was pounding so hard, it was a wonder he couldn't hear it. He was saying everything she'd dreamed of hearing. And as she looked into his eyes, she realized that now the decision was hers. He'd come to her. Told her he loved her—which she was still hugging close to her heart—and he wanted her. But uprooting her life wouldn't be easy. Her business. Her home.

As if he could read her mind, and hey, maybe today he could, he said, "You can open a new shop in Laguna. Or you can just keep this one and we'll all come to Utah every month so you can stay on top of things. We'll add on to your tiny house of course. But we all loved being here in the mountains. And we all love you. I love you."

She'd never get tired of hearing that, Lilah thought.

He held on to her and pulled her a bit closer. "I swear to you, Lilah, I will be the husband you deserve." His voice dropped to a husky rasp. "I will give you my word to be with you always. And I never break my word."

*Husband?* She swayed again. "You're proposing?"

He frowned. "Didn't I say that already? No. I didn't. I swear, just looking into your eyes empties my brain." He grinned now and her heart turned over. "Yes, I'm proposing." He dug into his pocket, pulled out a small black velvet jewelry box and flipped it open to reveal a canary yellow diamond ring.

"Oh, God..." She blew out a sigh and looked up at him through tear-blurred eyes.

"Marry me, Lilah. Live with me. Love with me. Make children with me—they'll grow up with Micah and Rosie and we'll love them so much they'll never doubt how precious they are to us.

"Between us, we'll build a family so strong, nothing can tear it apart." He bent, kissed her hard, fast. "I just need you to take a chance on me, Lilah. Risk everything. With me."

Lilah inhaled sharply and tried to ease the wild racing of her heart. But it was impossible. Her heart was his and it would always race when she was with him.

Finally, she lifted her hands, cupped his face in hers and whispered, "Love isn't a risk, Reed. Not when it's real. Not when it's as strong as our love is."

He turned his face and kissed her palm.

"I love you more than anything," she said softly. "Yes, I'll marry you and make children with you and love you forever. And I swear, we'll never get a divorce because I will *never* let you go."

He sighed and gave her another wide smile. "That is the best news I've ever heard."

Pulling the ring from the box, he slid it onto her finger, then kissed it as if to seal it into place. When she laughed in delight, he did, too, then he pulled her into his arms and kissed her, silently promising her a future, a life filled with love and laughter.

And all around them, the customers in the little shop applauded.

\* \* \* \* \*

# MILLS & BOON®
## Hardback – July 2016

## ROMANCE

| | |
|---|---|
| **Di Sione's Innocent Conquest** | Carol Marinelli |
| **Capturing the Single Dad's Heart** | Kate Hardy |
| **The Billionaire's Ruthless Affair** | Miranda Lee |
| **A Virgin for Vasquez** | Cathy Williams |
| **Master of Her Innocence** | Chantelle Shaw |
| **Moretti's Marriage Command** | Kate Hewitt |
| **The Flaw in Raffaele's Revenge** | Annie West |
| **The Unwanted Conti Bride** | Tara Pammi |
| **Bought by Her Italian Boss** | Dani Collins |
| **Wedded for His Royal Duty** | Susan Meier |
| **His Cinderella Heiress** | Marion Lennox |
| **The Bridesmaid's Baby Bump** | Kandy Shepherd |
| **Bound by the Unborn Baby** | Bella Bucannon |
| **Taming Hollywood's Ultimate Playboy** | Amalie Berlin |
| **Winning Back His Doctor Bride** | Tina Beckett |
| **White Wedding for a Southern Belle** | Susan Carlisle |
| **Wedding Date with the Army Doc** | Lynne Marshall |
| **The Baby Inheritance** | Maureen Child |
| **Expecting the Rancher's Child** | Sara Orwig |
| **Doctor, Mummy...Wife?** | Dianne Drake |

# MILLS & BOON®
## Large Print – July 2016

## ROMANCE

| | |
|---|---|
| The Italian's Ruthless Seduction | Miranda Lee |
| Awakened by Her Desert Captor | Abby Green |
| A Forbidden Temptation | Anne Mather |
| A Vow to Secure His Legacy | Annie West |
| Carrying the King's Pride | Jennifer Hayward |
| Bound to the Tuscan Billionaire | Susan Stephens |
| Required to Wear the Tycoon's Ring | Maggie Cox |
| The Greek's Ready-Made Wife | Jennifer Faye |
| Crown Prince's Chosen Bride | Kandy Shepherd |
| Billionaire, Boss...Bridegroom? | Kate Hardy |
| Married for Their Miracle Baby | Soraya Lane |

## HISTORICAL

| | |
|---|---|
| The Secrets of Wiscombe Chase | Christine Merrill |
| Rake Most Likely to Sin | Bronwyn Scott |
| An Earl in Want of a Wife | Laura Martin |
| The Highlander's Runaway Bride | Terri Brisbin |
| Lord Crayle's Secret World | Lara Temple |

## MEDICAL

| | |
|---|---|
| A Daddy for Baby Zoe? | Fiona Lowe |
| A Love Against All Odds | Emily Forbes |
| Her Playboy's Proposal | Kate Hardy |
| One Night...with Her Boss | Annie O'Neil |
| A Mother for His Adopted Son | Lynne Marshall |
| A Kiss to Change Her Life | Karin Baine |

# MILLS & BOON®
## Hardback – August 2016

## ROMANCE

| | |
|---|---|
| **The Di Sione Secret Baby** | Maya Blake |
| **Carides's Forgotten Wife** | Maisey Yates |
| **The Playboy's Ruthless Pursuit** | Miranda Lee |
| **His Mistress for a Week** | Melanie Milburne |
| **Crowned for the Prince's Heir** | Sharon Kendrick |
| **In the Sheikh's Service** | Susan Stephens |
| **Marrying Her Royal Enemy** | Jennifer Hayward |
| **Claiming His Wedding Night** | Louise Fuller |
| **An Unlikely Bride for the Billionaire** | Michelle Douglas |
| **Falling for the Secret Millionaire** | Kate Hardy |
| **The Forbidden Prince** | Alison Roberts |
| **The Best Man's Guarded Heart** | Katrina Cudmore |
| **Seduced by the Sheikh Surgeon** | Carol Marinelli |
| **Challenging the Doctor Sheikh** | Amalie Berlin |
| **The Doctor She Always Dreamed Of** | Wendy S. Marcus |
| **The Nurse's Newborn Gift** | Wendy S. Marcus |
| **Tempting Nashville's Celebrity Doc** | Amy Ruttan |
| **Dr White's Baby Wish** | Sue MacKay |
| **For Baby's Sake** | Janice Maynard |
| **An Heir for the Billionaire** | Kat Cantrell |

# MILLS & BOON®
## Large Print – August 2016

## ROMANCE

| | |
|---|---|
| The Sicilian's Stolen Son | Lynne Graham |
| Seduced into Her Boss's Service | Cathy Williams |
| The Billionaire's Defiant Acquisition | Sharon Kendrick |
| One Night to Wedding Vows | Kim Lawrence |
| Engaged to Her Ravensdale Enemy | Melanie Milburne |
| A Diamond Deal with the Greek | Maya Blake |
| Inherited by Ferranti | Kate Hewitt |
| The Billionaire's Baby Swap | Rebecca Winters |
| The Wedding Planner's Big Day | Cara Colter |
| Holiday with the Best Man | Kate Hardy |
| Tempted by Her Tycoon Boss | Jennie Adams |

## HISTORICAL

| | |
|---|---|
| The Widow and the Sheikh | Marguerite Kaye |
| Return of the Runaway | Sarah Mallory |
| Saved by Scandal's Heir | Janice Preston |
| Forbidden Nights with the Viscount | Julia Justiss |
| Bound by One Scandalous Night | Diane Gaston |

## MEDICAL

| | |
|---|---|
| His Shock Valentine's Proposal | Amy Ruttan |
| Craving Her Ex-Army Doc | Amy Ruttan |
| The Man She Could Never Forget | Meredith Webber |
| The Nurse Who Stole His Heart | Alison Roberts |
| Her Holiday Miracle | Joanna Neil |
| Discovering Dr Riley | Annie Claydon |

# MILLS & BOON®

## Why shop at millsandboon.co.uk?

Each year, thousands of romance readers find their perfect read at millsandboon.co.uk. That's because we're passionate about bringing you the very best romantic fiction. Here are some of the advantages of shopping at www.millsandboon.co.uk:

* **Get new books first**—you'll be able to buy your favourite books one month before they hit the shops

* **Get exclusive discounts**—you'll also be able to buy our specially created monthly collections, with up to 50% off the RRP

* **Find your favourite authors**—latest news, interviews  and new releases for all your favourite authors and series on our website, plus ideas for what to try next

* **Join in**—once you've bought your favourite books, don't forget to register with us to rate, review and join in the discussions

Visit **www.millsandboon.co.uk**
for all this and more today!